A MISPLACED WOMAN

A Novel of Courage in Verse

BY MARCY HEIDISH

A MISPLACED WOMAN
A Novel of Courage in Verse

Copyright © 2016 by Marcy Heidish

**LIBRARY OF CONGRESS
CATALOGING-IN-PUBLICATION DATA**
Heidish, Marcy.

p.cm.
ISBN: 978-0-9905262-5-4
Library of Congress Control Number: 2016952964

Cover: Vincent Willem van Gogh, "The Railway Bridge over Avenue Montmajour, Arles; Oil on canvas,71.0 x 92.0 cm., Arles: October, 1888; public domain

D&A (Dolan & Associates) Publisher
Printed in the United States of America
....
First edition

A MISPLACED WOMAN

A Novel of Courage in Verse

This Book Is For

The Homeless Women Who Inspired It

And

In Memory of
Sister Mary Ann Luby
Friend, Guide, Mentor
Who Inspired Me

CONTENTS

PROLOGUE

My Home Is in My Shoes

In sleep I hasten one more day.
I summon dawn, night's distant edge.
This city's maze awaits my tread.
My shoes know how to find the way.

For years, I lived in my old car.
It died after a faithful life.
I moved into a cardboard box
but it blocked the morning star.

Then, alone, I became my home.
My tough skin turned into walls.
This flesh clung to a fragile frame.
The rooftop was my skull's hard bone.

I was sheet-rock and two-by-fours
settled on these legs, this rump.
I lived one moment at a time
until the shelters offered more.

For many years I've lived in them:
three for the night, one for the day.
I can't call this the perfect life
but it may become a Bethlehem.

Today a vendor offered me a plum.
I saw this as hope's signature.
That purple juice, oh God, what joy.
Now I smell it on my thumb.

I chant these words when I take rest.
They are my anthem and my prayer
for strength along the traveler's road.
My shoes will guide me on my quest.

ONE

So Tell Me

"What the hell happened to you?"
A distant friend demands.
"You kind of disappeared."

"I felt called to be a nun," I joke.
She is startled, as I'd hoped.
"You're kidding," she says.

"Or maybe a test pilot," I add.
Her eyes narrow at me.
"Why tease?" She asks.

"I don't want to talk about it."
I smile, turn, back away.
"Call me." She waves.

When I was newly homeless,
I did not tell anyone.
Not anyone I knew.

And I stopped knowing them.
My other life peeled off
like old wet clothes.

This one wouldn't last too long,
I told myself each day.
Not for me, no way.

Everyone thinks this at first;
I didn't understand it.
Many of us never do.

First you are a girlish glacier,
next a solid block of ice,
then the melt begins.

You go from flood to puddle,
shrinking in the sun
until you are mist.

Drops of you stay in the air
or fall as dew at dawn,
or dapple a girl's hair.

By some mystery, over time,
your drops reunite again,
solidifying as a ghost,

but you'll never be the same
even when flesh returns,
you're forever changed.

How did my meltdown start?
I often wonder that.
Where? When?

It was on an ordinary night
in my father's house;
I think it was then.

Meltdowns may be violent,
subtle, slow, but
no one is exempt.

Who I Am Now

I am a misplaced woman
ghosting my way about the city

maybe glancing in a store,
maybe haunting quiet parks.

Since I pass along unnoticed,
my gloves need not match.
That's a snip of freedom.
Isn't it?

I am a displaced woman,
coasting my way about the city

maybe watching men walk by
maybe noticing a handshake.

Since I am invisible,
my hands need not match.
That's a nip of freedom.
Isn't it?

I am an erased woman
floating my way about the city

maybe without destinations,
maybe without places to go.

Since I am not heard,
my ears need not match.
That's a blip of freedom.
Isn't it?

I am a replaced woman
toting myself about the city

Since I don't "look homeless,"
(I have a locker for my stuff)
that's a drip of freedom.
Isn't it?

I am a reflected woman
noting myself in a mirror:

A redhead with some gray,
skin like a dog-eared page
in a twice-loaned paperback.

Dark eyes pained — but sane.
That's a sip of freedom.
Isn't it?

Well, isn't it?

Guess.

In This Life

In this life I have a pathway of cement,
a web of crossed and crossing streets,
a backpack and a bag of worn laments,

sometimes a pal to walk about with me;
soup kitchens, I know where they are.
I drag an unseen tail, a line of memories.

Nights, I have the star-like city lights,
a can of mace, a wary eye, a rapid step,
a fierce face and, of course, hindsight.

Once I was a student steeped in books.
Those vanished years serve me well:
Now I murmur poetry, once overlooked.

I think myself back into that other time:
leaves whispering, the pensive library,
its hidden shelves of words and rhymes.

In this life I hide stories under my cot,
I sleep on lines of iambic pentameter,
waking to that music I thought I forgot.

Across the avenues commuters rush by,
never guessing what's behind my face,
writing off what's written in my eyes.

I look at people on their way to work
I wonder what occupies their minds:
meetings, old clients, new customers?

Maybe they worry about a slow drain;
perhaps the rush of an urban avenue
mutes the secret murmur of a quatrain.

Do we share the same mental purse?
The man who sweeps past me now
may be a hidden kinsman in verse.

And maybe not at all, maybe not ever.
We know little of each other's depths,
even our own peculiar inner weather.

Meanwhile I move on, still hoping,
not for a hot meal or a bed just now;
but a life that arcs above mere coping.

It Comes Back

A night smoother than a black silk gown
spreads its skirts outside the open window.

Gold grilled cheese on a pearl-white plate,
a clear goblet jeweled with red wine:
formal colors in my father's house.

Every crust, each slice of grainy bread,
the gleam of the glass table before me,
my own fingerprints on an ivory napkin:

all appears sharp-edged, indelible, rich,
in my memory's most sacred niche.

I see this room as if from the rafters above:
The red circle of wine, almonds in a bowl,
my auburn mop of hair reflected in the glass.

As I drain the wine, push back the plate,
I note a candle, tulips, books on saints.

The dark kitchen crouches like a cave,
a convincing imitation of security.

I hear nothing ominous; I see nothing move
except the curtsies of my candle's flame;
the night is now a tender membrane.

Beyond I sense the city's darkened roofs,
But I don't sense the tall figure of my uncle
upstairs where he smokes, pacing, planning;

tanned, urbane, unencumbered by a wife,
he waits to crack a door and crush my life.

Shattering

I guess I went a little crazy
after my uncle caught me in the bath.
I was naked, nineteen, and naïve.

He drew my slick body out of the tub,
then drew himself down upon me.
I thought for a moment he had fallen.

When I knew what was happening
I stopped breathing except in gasps
as I stared up at the pale ceiling.

I didn't know why he was visiting
or how he found me upstairs alone
but it didn't matter and I didn't care.

I cared about making him stop it
but he was too strong too heavy so
I closed my eyes to make this not be.

He spread my legs apart just then
but I squeezed my eyelids tighter shut
until I turned myself into a shadow.

My eyes opened when I heard a cough,
a nervous cough from the hall beyond;
I'd heard it throughout my life.

My father stood there in the doorway
his bearish bulk outlined by the light
as he watched us down on the floor.

Not one word did my father speak
nor did he move into the room.
I tried but couldn't read his face.

I think now he was deep in shock.
"Never happened." His voice shook.
His brother panted, "Never. Ever."

My uncle lay there on top of me.
Footsteps echoed down the stairs.
"Can't breathe...." I whispered.

"Then don't." My uncle stood up,
shrugging on his Italian suit.
"Who'd believe you anyway?"

He left me there on the tiled floor.
The room spun in slow circles,
a merry-go-round breaking down.

That night I took my money,
packed a pair of suitcases and
left my father angry letters.

I quit his beautiful house.
I quit college and Washington.
I quit my old roots in that place.

Then I ran, not knowing where,
not knowing what to do next,
until a man saw his opportunity.

Cold Tiles

If you are raped
when you are raped
your mind floats away
on a silent journey
entirely on its own

It rises to the curtains
breathing gently
in a summer breeze
there you mind rests
in the cloth's safety

Then skims the ceiling,
your weightless mind,
above the man's heaving
back, sweat-stained,
erasing your body

Crushing its lovely ribs
leaving untouched
its slender white feet
its arms flung wide
as an open umbrella

Once he lumbers off
a slim instant later
only then your mind
like a silk scarf
floats back into you

Under your back
you feel the cold tiles
of the bathroom floor
where you had to
leave your body behind

You lie there how long?
No one can tell you
not your winged mind
the knobs of your spine
those curtains that saw

You will always be there
even after you leave
invisibly fastened to
that time, that space,
that clean ivory floor.

Moving On

We bruise
and we are bruised.
Some bruises last,
tattooed on the brain.

They're fused
to your anatomy
like head on neck
like flesh on bone.

When I ran away,
forever disowned,
wed, then alone,
I sold all I owned:

Tall candlesticks,
rings, bracelets,
anything of gold:
my hidden trove.

I lived in my car,
buying gas, food,
my license plates
for several years.

This can be done
with sparing care;
it all fades finally
except old bruises.

You accept them
with passing time;
they don't change
with effort or age.

Follow Your Heart

Follow your heart
whenever it calls to you
wherever it tells you to go...

Don't do it. That's one thing you can't allow.
Don't believe the words of crooners' songs.
I did that, years ago — look at me now.

Listen. I know what I'm talking about.
Use your head, but, please, not your heart.
Mine has the knowhow of a waterspout.

It advised me to drop out of college,
run off with a soldier — oh so classic —
who took my money and his booze.

I hardly knew him, never missed him.
He was overseas most of the time;
at home, he was heavy into drinking.

Proud, angry, I would not go home,
I stuck it out at a distant army post,
never wrote, called, asked for help.

Father, in a rage, soon disowned me,
cut all ties as I was treading water.
My head told me to get a clerk's job

but my heart told me to be a writer.
I'd get published and show them all.
After six years I was broke and lonely.

That's enough of my sob-story for now.
All of us have one, mine's hardly novel.
I will not sing the blues nor show you how.

I tell you this only to warn you well:
your heart can be a heartless deceiver,
leading you on a flowered path to Hell.

On the Frontier

I am living in a different country now
without a passport or a visa or a permit.
I didn't notice when I crossed the border
though I knew this was different terrain.
I thought I made a detour when I came
but stayed so long I became a citizen.
The language sounds almost the same;
a few small variations, nothing more.
I traveled on a one-way road, I heard.
Few make it back to where they were.
This city must be right on the frontier
of a Nowhere and a Somewhere else.

Everything is different but the same,
as if I'm always standing on my head,
looking at the world from an odd angle.
Maybe it's the *world* that's upside-down
and I'm standing on my own two feet.
Nobody can tell me which is which
but someone must know what to do.
Years have passed but I am the same.
Odd, that's how I feel, a stranger still,
though I can act as if I do belong here.
It's best, I think, to look like a native.

Upside down may be right side up,
but I gave up figuring all this out.
Instead I found a way to come and go.
With that I make it through the day.
People treat me as if I am a foreigner,
always on the margins of the page —
not inside the black chunks of print.
Sometimes I wonder if I'm cursed
but I just look away if I am jeered.
If I can't find a road that goes back,
I'll become a Someone here between
Nowhere and Somewhere. I'll survive.

A Donated Apple

Don't pity me. Don't you dare.
I own part of an orchard now,
a fruit vendor's gift to me today.
This apple, like me, is homeless,
separated from its family of trees,
but it blooms like a rose in my hand;
no self-pity found in its rounded form.
I love to feel an apple's flavored heft,
its hidden flesh, a surprising white,
waiting under its sexy red dress.
I recite some of its many tribal names:
Granny Smith, Red Delicious, McIntosh:
the words taste tart/sweet on my tongue.
Of course this apple is slightly bruised
like most of this vendor's offerings to us,
but who isn't bruised a little or a lot?
That vendor can't guess the meaning
of such gifts to my street-sisters; to me.
They get us through the afternoons,
that long stretch of heat or cold or rain,
when the midday demons whisper to us,
You really screwed up your life, didn't you?
That is when we reach for stale cigarettes
or a few reach for that bottle in a paper bag.
This day I reach deep inside my backpack
to draw out with reverence — my apple.

Soup Kitchen

Through the dusk, through the rain,
I watch some thirty women gather,
a long tangled line down the street.
Heads bend, lift, stay stiff as icons.
Scarves, bandanas, baseball caps.
Shoulders shifting, shrug, straighten,
wrapped in dry cleaners' plastic bags
to keep off glistening strings of rain.

Below is a collection of restless feet;
boots, sneakers stuffed with paper.
I take my place at the back of the line.
This bright soup kitchen opens soon
for the dinner we thought of all day.
Hands thrust deep into pockets, armpits.
Suddenly, the door swings open wide,
the women begin to file their way inside.

The building used to be a private school,
closed when the neighborhood changed.
This shelter has traces of the place it was.
Walls, painted with pilgrims, stay bright.
On the windows, outlines of pasted leaves.
And on the blackboard in the dining room,
someone has chalked, *This Places Sucks*.
Under that a new notation: *Think of Me!*

Smell of wet hair, wet wool, cooked food.
The platters are ready at the serving station.
Steam rising: Mac'N Cheese, Mac'N Cheese.
An older white women, Lil, moves along.
Fork. Spoon. Napkin. Blood-red Kool-Aid.
Cigarette clamped in her teeth, smoke rising.
Her table cloaked in red-checked plastic.
Lil, impish, wise, dark-haired, sits at last.

A black woman, gnarled as ancient trees,
raps the floor three times with her cane.
"That my place," she barks and raps again.
Lil moves over one, avoiding a "ruction."
Nearby, tented in a milky blanket, sits Angel.
Rocking, she extends one elegant long hand.
Ma'am gives Angel a napkin, then feeds her.
The cane raps again. Together, we say Grace.

The rain outside sounds heavier right now.
Lightning sends a eerie flash into the room.
We're gathering our plastic wraps around us.
The streets will be watered down and slick
and the gutters will run with dark sludge.
I feel our dread; it hangs over each table.
We finish our food, saving our stale Oreos,
then dash out to the waiting cave of night.

At the Night Shelter

Blinking, I wake early here.
Windows frame a lemon dawn.

Stronger then, morning light lifts
eighteen sleepers from the dark.

I am a piece in a jigsaw puzzle of
mattresses on this chapel's floor,

all donated to the church that runs
this tight night-shelter for women.

We even have a map with names;
everyone knows who rests where.

Now we stir under thin blankets,
sunshine striping all our faces.

Waking, shaking heads, some say:
"Thank you, God, for another day."

Never a curse, often that prayer.
I still can't speak it and mean it.

Blankets folded, faces splashed,
we line up for coffee and rolls,

stale old rolls tasting so damn fine,
we're intent on tearing into them.

By seven, mattresses are stowed,
the chapel is cleaned, restored.

Over the altar, a purple felt banner:
I am the vine, you are the branches.

We must be out by seven-thirty sharp;
we trudge toward our hot-lunch place.

Our stuff, our bags, we leave all here,
locked in with the labeled mattresses.

More light, like butter melting over us.
No rain, salty clouds, a blue-eyed day.

The doorway widens in a yawn —
chill air slaps us, now fully awake.

"Shit," says someone. "Frozen tits."
"Thanks all the same, another day."

Out and About

The day opens around us
in the form of a street,
our Red Carpet,
our River Jordan,
our Road to Calvary —
all of these or some of these
depending on what day it is
and how you slept last night
and what the weather is like.

Who predicts weather like us?
We watch it as a farmer does,
planning every route we take
around skies and temperature.
We learn to sense it instantly
when we first hit the streets.
We had no early preparation.
Who dreams of growing up
to be a homeless woman?

Now I take myself to "my" café.
Almost every day I'm in there;
Many places do not let me in.
Only here I am not invisible.
Through the classy windows
I watch harried hurried people:
So many who seem unhappy,
and they actually have homes.
When I had one, did I frown?

Why didn't I throw myself down,
head bent, arms outstretched,
before the door of my house,
tears like pearls on my face,
keys chiming in my pockets
as I might greet an Archangel
or a lover returning from war,
and cried out, cried up to God,
O Hosanna in the Highest?

Why did I fail to do all that,
taking "home" for granted?
Why was I never warned:
I could turn out homeless.
Do those commuters get it?
one big fire, a bankruptcy,
a lost job, a long illness —
and the slide down begins.
I'd warn them to no avail.

Now this café guy I know
comes to my window seat,
his face open as an avocado,
freshly sliced, mellow, ripe.
"So what can I get for you?"
he asks although he knows.
"A French poodle," I kid him.
I have never been charged.
Not for one hot dark drink.

Maybe for a French poodle.

What Can I Get You?

My friend, a vendor, always asks.
I'll take a grape but I want to say:

Get me a pair of four-inch heels
  and an evening gown in ivory silk
  and an underwire bra that fits me
  and a facial made of avocado oil
  and a manicure with a classic red
  and a pedicure in a perfect match
  and a shampoo plus a conditioner
  and a full-bodied herbal massage
  and fresh water pearls for earrings
  and a choker necklace of the same
  and elbow-length ivory silk gloves
  and an onyx velvet evening cloak
  and a bottle-green Lincoln Sedan
  and a chauffeur in a tux and tails
  and a billionaire to be my escort
  and two fine box seats at the Met
  and a private jet to fly us there
  and a late supper at Le Cirque
  and my escort's life insurance
  and my name as beneficiary
  and his sudden painless death
  and a merry widowhood for me
  and a happy-ever-after lifetime
  and a bonus for the homeless
  and a home for all my friends
  and a mocha latte until then.

That's all.

Moving Out

Eviction is a blood sport,
not one for the faint of heart.
The city takes your things
but don't stay on to watch
your house fileted like a fish,
then scaled of all its silver.

Round as a good pancake,
the table was the first to go,
bringing with it ten birthdays,
twelve Easters, fifteen parties,
seven thousand hot breakfasts
and a partridge in a pear tree.

I still see the sofa lifted out
by three sweating workers
in red tee shirts, all printed:
"We Can Move Your Ass."
Then a team of six removes
the Steinway grand piano.

No, you can't take it with you.
The guts of a six-room home
won't fit into two backpacks.
You must begin over again:
For the young, that's hip-hop;
for the aging, that's aerobics.

You have to train for this one
but you're never quite ready.
There is the marital mattress,
borne aloft like a dead queen;
There, the naked bookshelves.
Here, the pier glass, cracked.

How it Ended

What I remember are the candlesticks,
their moon-silver gleam
still breaking through my cloudy dreams.

Next I remember one small side table,
left behind on the sidewalk;
the city had my furniture in its truck.

Left off were two chairs, the table,
the coat I was wearing
and two candlesticks in my hands.

It was four degrees on January fourth.
It was six or seven at night:
It was the season for evictions.

From a church came a stranger;
she brought bread, candles,
hot soup, but I could not eat then.

That night was cold enough to crack
but I kept on sweating
as I saw my life loaded on that rig.

Sure, I'd fallen behind in my rent
but I had another job lined up;
my landlord promised a month of grace.

His teeth looked like two white fences,
that false grin, that wink —
His lies led me to sit here on the street.

Now the stranger lit her paired candles;
they fingered the dark.
I resisted a strong and sudden urge to vomit.

This wasn't really happening, I thought.
I was not really sitting here.
No, I had risen into the frigid air above.

As we dined on the street, the table faded out,
only the candles remained.
The city's truck rolled off as if on roller skates.

I told the stranger I could not leave my things;
that was impossible.
I would stay with them through that cold night.

Just then, it seemed easy, freezing to death
outside my own home;
gently, in my own chair, I'd drift off to sleep.

The stranger set her hands on my shoulders.
She pinned me with a look.
It felt like a sharp needle piercing my cheek.

I gathered my handbag, my scarf, my wool hat.
Without glancing back,
I walked, my chin out, toward my own old car.

There I stowed a crammed backpack, two bags,
keys, clothes, pearls, ID.
When I'd been calmer, I'd salvaged such things.

I started the Chevy and stepped hard on the gas.
Somehow I was dead calm;
the street's white line my life-line, my guide-line.

I drove and drove, didn't know where, didn't care,
finally stopped in an alley
when street signs blurred; there I spent the night.

When I woke, the sun fell like God's gaze over me.
I could breathe, I'd survived.
At that moment, nothing else seemed to matter.

I felt for my cash, thermos, license — all of it there.
From here, I would go on.
I'd lived through the worst; like honey, grace flowed.

Wheels

When I lived in my ancient car
I always got a good night's sleep.

Over me the Chevy's roof floated,
a seamless canopy of bluish steel,

even under spiteful stones of hail,
vicious rains or merciless heat.

The back seat had stayed firm,
with exactly enough spring to it:

the bounce of a good pound cake,
while my steadfast canvas tarp

covered the car like tough skin,
calloused as a work-worn hand.

I learned where to park at dusk,
streets in safer neighborhoods,

different ones on different nights,
or hotels, motels, all-night lots,

when my car seemed like a boat
slipping into its familiar port.

In those days I was less afraid,
stupidly proud of my navigation,

knowing how to locate restrooms,
coffee hours, bar food, tastings —

I believed all of this would pass.
My worries? Running out of gas.

It's always like that at the start.

After My Chevy Nova Died

I lived with a gal, Roxy, in a box,
three by five, two shades of gray.

The "Cardboard Condominiums,"
our nearest neighbors liked to say.

It was a town of boxes, every size:
a home to me, that desperate day.

underneath a broadened bridge:
the bed for a busy expressway.

We heard cars' constant *whoosh*,
their accelerations, their delays,

throughout our fractured sleeps,
our dreamlike communal haze,

except when we greeted the sun,
far above that rat-invested Hades.

As a pair we searched for bread
on our frequent, fruitful forays,

raiding Dumpsters to find cookies,
pizza crusts; so much thrown away.

A bottle cut Roxy's arm one time.
Bloodied, both of us, we prayed.

She laid cobwebs in her wound.
It acted as gauze, she was okay.

Sparrows in an outgrown nest,
we had no eggs to eat or lay.

except what we could dig up —
we were cashless castaways.

Roxy traded daily sex for drugs,
to take the edge off, she'd say.

In her eyes the lights were out.
She gulped pills: "I gotta play."

Asleep we smelled each other:
skin, hair, rags; I couldn't stay.

And so I quit cardboard boxes,
trash fires, roaches on display.

I see Roxy's black beauty still.
As I left, she hollered, "Hooray."

Steam Heat

If you have to sleep out on the street
when the temperature hits seventeen,
remember to lay cardboard down first,
with a good-sized blanket to top it.
Then you lie down in all your clothes,
stuffed with newspapers, of course,
and pull one more blanket over you
and anything else you've picked up:
oil cloth, canvas, an old tablecloth.
Chances are you'll live to see morning.

Steam grates scald but often work.
I know a man who claims a grate,
sleeping on his chosen one for years.
He's been beaten up at bus stations;
fights break out in shelters, he says.
He likes the freedom of having a grate.
The wind is more deadly than the cold.
If you want to check out, take the wind.
You learn this first; you learn it fast.
I tell you this because you never know.

Who'd think a girl from a "good family,"
a fine house, private schools, of course,
her father a lawyer, servants at home,
would run from an Ivy League college,
kick around from bad job to bad job,
wed a man who would take her money
and, ten years later, sleep on a grate?
Sounds like Cinderella run in reverse.
That's my story but I don't tell it now,
not to the people who live in my world.

I was throttled by a female wrestler,
homeless, after listening to my tale.
"You chucked it all, you dumb bitch?"
I tried to explain but she roared again.
"Disinherited? Shit. No pity from me."
After that, I've kept things to myself.
But at night when the demons arrive,
I hear that roar of a voice in my head.
"You chucked it all, you dumb bitch?"
I hear those words in the daylight, too.

The Enemy

January is the Devil's month,
cold enough to freeze you dead,
merciless as hatred to confront.

A deceiver, winter seems angelic,
cloaked in the pale purity of snow,
— and seductive as a psychedelic.

For my mates, winter is an enemy,
numbing our fingers, feet, and faces,
dropping us into Gethsemane.

There temperatures can be deadly
if shelters fill and trash fires are few.
Get arrested or go into free-fall.

Underneath a bridge, you wait
to live or die, the choice to make
or you tell yourself it's up to Fate.

Sun-up: Disappointment or relief?
You rise, you move; kitchens open.
Drink hot coffee; swallow your grief.

I think of going home to my father
but no, too much anger, pain.
I'll never go back, begging.

I bore winter's brunt one year,
after my eviction, and I swear:
January *is* the Devil's month.

On the Street Where I Live

"Get the hell off my grate," shouts Meg,
then grins when she sees it's me.
"Sorry, pal. Some newcomer there."

It is known: Meg "owns" this grate,
only sharing it with me one winter,
after I had left the box under the bridge.

The place is off the mainline routes.
Cops around here look the other way,
so Meg is "comfortable," as she insists.

She gets donated food from local grocers;
water from a nearby hose or hydrant,
wraps her cart in black garbage bags.

Sixty, tough, with one long silver braid,
she scoffs at winter, summer, rain, hail,
and all the shelters for homeless women.

"A box," I say now, just to rile her up.
"They're clean, no fights, no fuss —"
Her look could strip the paint off walls.

"The hell I will," she barks. "Not ever."
She stretches like a bather on a beach.
"Got my freedom here, won't trade it in."

Grate-squatters are a distinct breed,
fiercely independent, no rules or boss.
"A Cardboard Condo," she spits again.

I think of Meg, her squatter's rights
but they don't tempt me; never will.
"Women are so vulnerable," I tell her.

"You with your big words, college girl."
She winks at me. "Vulnerable? Shit."
Meg would be a pioneer in another age.

I can see her with a rifle on a horse,
a stallion, black, no saddle, only guts.
At night, her hard face comes to mind.

She's in her bedroll, this city cowgirl.
One eye open, she can go to sleep.
Meg drifted in from Idaho, somehow.

She does not talk much about that
but it made Meg pretty damn tough;
Mostly, she refuses to remember.

Does she dream of the logger she left?
He hit her, she hit back, that was it.
I think she dreams of open prairies.

So the street becomes her own plains,
her grate's her land, her frontier home,
steaming like an old-time wood-stove.

"Won't have it no other way," she says.
At night Meg rides the range she craves.
By day she blazes trails through trees.

I don't know why she stays in the city.
"Faster than the west, rougher, too,"
she tries explaining to her "college girl."

For me there are few friends like Meg.
Staunch, loyal, she's not afraid to die.
"I'll go with my boots on. But will you?"

Dirty Dancing

If you wanted a good bath, you went to Union Station.
So I learned those months I tried living on the streets.

At that time the train station's huge Women's Room
was fit for thorough sponging if you weren't modest;
if you came at night, if some insider let you stay.

I can see the way we looked reflected in the mirrors:
Women reveling in their self-laundered status.

I remember: flash of bodies, lather, water, steam.
Smell of donated shampoo, cheap donated soap;
some women washing with big handfuls of *Tide*.

Flash of flesh: breasts, bellies, thighs, feet, necks,
scrubbed and dried, bit by bit, then covered again.

The opening of every wash-night dance was this:
foot in sink, steady, first the left, then the right.
Swing one leg up, do it good, don't skip your bum.

Afterwards, I felt like fresh linen, ironed, too,
as I strode out through the city's gritty avenues.

Now I'm in a place where there are showers.
The feel of heated water on your back, I hear,
is a damn sight better than springtime or sex.

Still, sometimes I miss our hours at the station,
washing up as trains churned through the night.

Coming Home

I bathe my face in the baptismal font,
early, when the church is empty,
sometimes on a saint's day, maybe not.
The sexton, a friend, stands sentry.

The church, I feel, invites me to come in.
I smell wax, carnations, floor polish
in the only place I've ever felt at home;
all else has broken down, demolished.

I still hear the click of Rosary beads:
that sound, for me, a consecration
written on thin air only God can read
sifting down through generations.

For now, I am where I always belong,
here my harbor, here my mooring,
here, in gratitude, I would fall headlong
while my spirit flies high, soaring.

Now I am not an outcast on my knees.
When I grab His hem, it's me He sees.

TWO

Social Worker's Intake Report, April 22, 1985

Subject:
Andromeda Lane, Female Caucasian, age 34
AKA "Andie"

A daily "regular:"
Gilead Shelter for Homeless Women
April 21, 1985–the present

Vital Statistics
Born to Gilbert & Rose Lane, March 17,1951
Rose Lane d. 1951
Raised by "more than a nanny," Tess Moran
Married 1969; Divorced 1980

Note on Background:
Wealthy home
Washington, DC
Roman Catholic

General Health: Good

Psych Health: Normal, as tested
No drugs, alcohol

Reasons for Homelessness:
Savings stolen by spouse
Disowned by father
No living relatives
Low-pay jobs (writing)

Career:
Freelance editor, writer
Waitress, messenger

General History:
    Runaway at 19 years of age
    Lived in own car, 6+ yrs
    Lived on streets, 2 yrs

Note:
Sexual Trauma, age 19
Will not discuss

Notes:
    Ready for Transitional Housing
    None available at this time

Gilead Shelter for Women

I slept in clean night-shelters
    but the days were long and empty.

Hungry, I rummaged in the Dumpsters;
    Was I slowly turning into an animal?

Then I discovered this new house,
    This day-shelter I'd heard about,

    just in time for Gilead's hot lunch,
my nose blue with cold, cheeks flushed,

    fingernails rimmed with black —
they knew I'd lived on the streets.

Smiling at the floor, I stood still,
    shy as a child on school's first day,

but something set me into motion.
    "Thank you," I told everyone —

then "Thank you," to the heater,
    to the chairs, to the wooden tables

in the dining room, more "Thanks"
    as we sat down to a hot lunch.

I offered my gratitude again when
    they said Grace; I chanted "Amen."

My eyes filled as I smelled hot food.
    The women ignored my street-grime.

Someone passed me a loaded plate.
    Finally, I wiped my wet face. I ate.

Dream House

Maybe I dreamed that it spoke,
the voice of this ancient house,
the Gilead Day Shelter for Women,
and maybe this is what it said:

"I am far more than a house
surely you know that by now.
Call me creaky cross shabby
but after all I am an old lady.

"I tilt toward the future
out of the past to shelter you
but I've had a life of my own
before you came here to me:

"Godmother to thirty or so
the governess of nineteen
my guarding roof spread
across three generations.

"It was not so easy for me
to keep out the rainstorms,
expel those persistent mice,
keep a look-out for burglars.

"I had to remain quite alert
to the pranks of small boys,
the careless use of matches,
cigarettes and awful cigars.

"Built in 1905, I've survived
some abuse, some neglect,
but I refuse any complaints,
after all, I am still standing.

"When I was sold I fretted
but I received a new family.
You girls come and go but
I'm home to everyone here.

"My protection goes out to
those longtime regulars,
and those passing through:
This, my greatest vocation.

"Remember, I am genteel,
though my finery is worn.
I was raised as a hostess,
gracious, welcoming to all

"but I surpass that role now.
Late in life, I am a mother.
May others like me appear:
More of me: that is my prayer."

Shelter: Front Yard

Weeds, wet, rise like harp strings.
Trying out their morning voices,
birds begin to clear their throats.

The sun, a yellow plate, serves us
the morning from Eastern skies
while cobwebs glitter on a hedge.

Hold it! Stay this way, don't move,
I shout, but days can't be detained,
they rush into gray business suits.

That crevice between night and day,
liminal, magical, impractical, is gone
into the crisp offices of working hours.

All day I'll look ahead to twilight;
I wear its colors woven as a shawl.
At last, the light begins to change.

Soon a thimble of time will spill
its liquid lavenders into this yard;
I will know it's there if I am not.

Lilac dusk, wedge of moon, a star;
jaws of jagged rooftops bite the sky.
A river of ink flows into the dark.

Which instant to catch if I could paint?
The city's night or the city's evening?
My brush would dip into the lavender.

Washing Dishes at the Shelter

A fire is caught in that tree there,
scattering sparks into the street.
Sunlight flames through the maple
as if this tree is about to burn down,
but it moves like a living creature
trying to shake free of its own blaze.

I'm washing dishes in the kitchen window
of the Gilead Shelter for Homeless Women.
I'm a regular here for the daily hot lunch,
"hanging-out" space; trees across the way.
A nun in jeans runs the place, runs it well.
"No time for tears," she says. "No tears."

The world is wild, crazy, dangerous, sure,
but Sister Nan keeps a clean, orderly house.
Here, being homeless is not exactly a shocker.
We're all alike, but at Gilead we have names.
Now I look at that maple and see each of us,
trying to shake off our own private blazes.

We don't speak of them, we just keep going:
Full-time work, no holidays, begging, sobs.
"Get a job, bitch," a guy yelled at me once;
"Got a job," I hollered. "It's called survival."
Then I shut up. You can't let in stuff like that.
You need all your strength to make it through.

So I watch the trees and I watch my back and
I watch the transvestite prostitutes in the alley.
On this street we're interested in staying alive.
When the leaves fall, branches pattern the sky.
If rain brews, we get dry cleaners' plastic bags.
To scatter red leaves, you protect your trunk.

Leaves

Dance in the light.
Let your falling leaves scatter.
Don't rake them too soon.

The angel is here in his truck.
His baseball cap and his boots
make him look like a workman
but you know what he is.

His blower swirls the leaves.
They rise upward like kites.
Paste their colors to the sky
before they plummet down.

If a blue moose comes out
of the woods to eat leaves
welcome him as your guest.
Let him look into your face.

Look back at him and leap.
Whirl in the yellow leaves
while you can. Dance.

After Mopping the Kitchen Floor

I walked through the shelter's back door
only to wring out our tired string mop

when a cloud of them rose around me
like bright flower petals in flight —

a swarm of butterflies I'd disturbed,
swirling, circling my head, my hair,

offering me a faint thrumming sound
firm but frail as an infant's eyelids.

I thought of all of my absent friends
coming to me in these fluttering forms,

brushing my face as if in a greeting,
reminding me they were still out there —

and then the swarm turned and was gone
leaving me with the mop still in my hand

its insistent drip-drip my song of thanks.

Brutal Beauty

Set against a dawning sky,
the dark shape is elegant,
etched precisely, as if inked
on a banner, stiff and pale,
hanging from the clothesline
stretched across an alley.

On the air I trace the lines
of this bold black profile:
spare, simple, mysterious,
the figure appears to me as
last night's present left for us,
thrilled by all small glories.

What artist made this image?
A young girl with secret talent
or a janitor who lives to paint?
I wipe the shelter's window,
smudged by too much smoke,
so I can get the clearest view.

I move closer now, squinting,
and rush out to look again.
I cross the street, stop short
and look and look and look.
It is a dead cat, tailless, black,
hanging from the clothesline.

Is this the work of a drunk
or a kid playing a sick prank?
I'll never know but I know this:
Brutal beauty isn't new to us.
The lovely and the lurid mix.
Why should I be so shaken?

Why I Don't Do Drugs

My life's a thread; I want to keep it on the spool.

I've seen how fast threads can start unraveling,
until they knot and twist into a tangle on the floor.

When threads fade, their clear lines get crossed,
and soon no one can find a start or an ending.

Sometimes a thread can shred or break apart
or become the frayed strands of a wet mop
or a fiddle's broken strings, dangling in the air.

That's how it would be for me, of that I'm sure.
I don't want to lose my way or worse, myself,
what's left of them, so I stay wrapped and tight.

I can still pass through the eye of a used needle
I'm still strong enough to form worthy stitches
and hold a hem up if that's what I have to do.

When I'm stored I know which choice to make:
I wind myself around that tiny wooden spindle.

Dull as that may seem, it's safer than dazzle.

In the Park

I wonder how the broad lawns feel
spreading themselves beneath us.
Our footprints leave darker marks
like small shadows on the grasses
and oh the green of them so deep
so tolerant so tremulous so tender
— the park decides to welcome us.

We run rest roam ramble rejoice,
if we remember how rejoicing goes,
and there in Montrose park we can,
for the span of a one May afternoon
when the sun calls a big *Yes* to us:
come on come out come over here.

What woman can say *No* to the sun
when it leads us out of the streets
beyond city cement, beyond asphalt;
not for long not for days or forevers,
just between lunchtime and dinner
when the skies open their windows.

I sit on a worn bench in sliced light
its wood as warm as an open hand;
there I can write down what I see
and use big words without a tease
the blades of grass reach up to me
whispering I can be who I must be.

Here we are all free Somebodies.
Flowers reveal new blooms to us,
allowing us to see into their eyes
within the circled skin-like petals.
We stare at each fragile mystery
before church bells strike three.

Gilead's Invader

She picked it up by its scaly tail —
the dead rat, shaped like a man's shoe.

It hung there in the air
for half an hour
so it seemed
until she dropped it
with a dead thing's thud
into a black Hefty bag
then dumped it
in the outside trash.

"How'd" you learn that?"
We stared at Sister Nan.
"There are always rats."
Yes. We had forgotten.

"Maybe others?" Sue asked.
"Poisoned them," said Nan.

I thought of rats
you didn't recognize
but food was ready.

"Lunch," Nan called.
I set out the plates;
watched for rodents.

"Grace?" I asked.
We thanked God.
The women ate.
I looked for rats.

We cleared tables,
watched for rats,
refilled the cups,
watched for rats,
served pudding,
cleared, swept.
"Always, rats."

Yes. We knew.

The Challenge

The new woman was a birch tree,
six feet tall, skinny, white, too white.
Green hair sprouted from her head.
"My leaves, y'know." A bitter laugh.
After that, the birch tree didn't speak.

I saw her shooting up in our alley
once she did a business man or two.
Her pusher knew his time to come:
when the big shiny cars pulled out
and sped off, blending with the traffic.

When I raked the shelter's front yard,
it glimmered like silver in the sunlight.
Lovely, lush and luminous it seemed,
but I discovered what made the glint:
used needles, flung out into the night.

The day Birch mutinied was clear;
windows framed a blueberry sky.
As we began to serve noon lunch
Birch set her syringe on the table,
daring us, in silence, to scold her.

"Out," Sister Nan ordered Birch.
"Make me," the woman snapped.
"No drugs here, you know that,"
the nun snapped back. "Get out."
"Make me," Birch snarled again.

Sister Nan inched toward her as
Birch lashed out, her fists furled.
Quickly, Sister backed her off
with a chair, lifted, its legs out,
as lion-tamers sometimes do.

The nun got Birch out our door,
but the challenge was not over.
Birch stood on our porch where
she shot up, too fast, too much,
and fell dead on the sidewalk.

After 911 was called and came,
after the long body was bagged
after the police had gone away,
Sister Nan announced lunch.
"Eat," she said. "Stick to life."

You're So Great?

A girl from Hell's here.
Hating me: she loves it.
cheeks snowfall pale,
red sunrise her mouth,
black hair, black eyes,
watching me for weeks.

"Slumming?" She rasps.
Her hand on my throat,
her hissing in my ear.
"What —?" I'm choking.
"Slumming, Princess."
"Wrong," I'm gasping.
"Shut up, you bitch."

Around my head,
spinning faster,
questions zing
like buzzing flies.
Ask. Ask. Ask.
Not letting up.
Tell, tell, tell.

Face to face,
she bites me.

"So, Good Goody."
She shakes me.
"You don't booze.
You don't do dope.
You don't do men.
You don't do girls.
What do you do?"

"Die." Me, yelling.
"Die inside, I do.
"Try to wither,
numb myself,
hope not to feel,"
I'm telling her.
"Since the rape,
that's what I do."

This tames her.
Glad I hurt, too.

Crazy Bouquet

If I could see my life as a bouquet,
it would be a clutch of crazy colors,
lacking any definite arrangement,
wild but still artistic in its strangeness.

Blossoms from the places where I've lived
make up this wild and random fistful,
gathered by design or accident or both;
I never can be sure but does that matter?

I won't write these states' clever mottos
or the songs of every place I've been.
I have no photographs to paste in albums
but at each home I've pressed its flowers:

Here, the rose of my birthplace, New York,
tucked next to the Yucca of New Mexico,
needling the Massachusetts mayflower,
Tennessee's blue iris; Virginia's pink dogwood.

There, Maine's lone white pine cone, nestles
Colorado's columbine, Arizona's saguaro;
the yellow black-eyed Susan of Maryland
and the Bluebonnet of Texas rounds it out.

My bouquet is mostly reds and pinks,
some golds, spiked with cactus and a cone.
Blurred together, they're a patchwork quilt,
a Pollack painting or a pepperoni pizza.

That's okay by me, I'm tired of tidiness.
A mess alone can make a masterpiece.

Upscale Voodoo

I still see that aging woman, hair salt-white,
frail but straight-backed in her navy-blue silk suit,
buttoned with the quiet gleam of distant stars.

Dividing the sidewalk a workmen's cable,
heightened by a metal sleeve, lay between us,
one to cross with a dancer's careful step.

As we neared this line, we faced each other,
this woman and I, as she hesitated, then halted.
I reached out to her with my right hand.

Without glancing up, her eyes fixed on the cable,
she took my hand and clung to it as she moved ahead,
taking one long stride: to her, it was a leap.

Only when I joined her did she look at me,
dressed carelessly in unmatched patchy shirts.
I saw fear flicker in her hazel gaze.

What upscale voodoo tipped that woman off?
Perhaps it was my clothing or my weathered face,
or an aura, undefinable, of poverty and loss.

I wanted to say, "We aren't all alike, you know."
I hoped to say, "Who cares what you think?"
Stupidly I said, "Did you go to Vassar, too?"

With eyes averted then, she dropped my hand.
I watched her as she walked off, never glancing back.
The instant evaporated, frozen only in my dreams.

How Cate Did it

The wooden stick was skinny as a straw,
the gum was pinker than a puppy's tongue.
Together, they formed an ingenious tool
in the slender hand of Catherine Healy
as she labored within her chosen church.

A generous Archangel of a sanctuary
spread its slate wings over Catherine
as she knelt beside the votive candles
in the nave, empty after morning mass.
Offering her prayers, she began to work.

Bubble gum was fixed to a stick's end,
slid through the slot within the Poor Box,
bringing forth a coin stuck to the gum.
On a good day, Catherine got quarters,
shining like scrubbed faces in her palm.

When the pastor caught her in the act,
Catherine rose, defiant, in the aisle.
"That's a Poor Box — and *I'm* the poor,"
she spoke up to the startled priest.
"Don't come back again," he yelled.

At dinner, we didn't laugh at Catherine.
We knew she felt homeless once again.
At the night-shelter, before Lights Out,
we stood around her, a circle of sisters,
trying to absorb her pain into our own.

Migration

Answers fly by with the birds.
And not only birds.
Wildebeests and bats and salmon,
they always knew it.

For years I watched Canadian geese,
wings beating the air over Maryland.
Now I see I learned little from them,
but they knew it, too.

Migration is bred into all creatures
so our plans to move on
are not eccentric, not new, not wild,
but why didn't we know it?

We are one with African wildebeasts,
Mexican bats, and Pacific salmon,
moving in their ancient patterns,
but why didn't we know it?

Homeless women migrate, too,
from street to street, shelter to shelter,
as we recast our backdrops, our sets,
but still we don't know it.

Who wants to be one with the salmon
who migrate to spawn and then die?
We're nearing our last upstream swim,
but who wants to know it?

Musings:
Does the Soul Need Pockets?

I think of death, of course,
more often than I did before.
Odd questions arise like this:

Does the soul need pockets?
After vacating its recent home,
the soul must start a silent journey.

It would have to pass checkpoints,
a requirement in absolute effect
for those who plan to travel on.

We can guess what is prohibited:
Sharp words, grudges, malice....
Prayers are tested for sincerity.

We think you may bring memories:
top choices are an infant's first cry;
embraces and faces of open joy.

Sunsets and seas are still popular;
aromas of coffee, cut grass, curries,
and always, carnal sighs, et cetera.

The topic of virtue is not discussed.
That's what we call a "gray area,"
addressed three levels higher up.

Likely, we can take three-ounce vials
as appropriate containers for Mercy;
two-inch tubes will do for Generosity.

The information I imagine now
should answer all my questions.
There is no box for suggestions.

My Doctor Is a Laptop

His name, I think, is Apple.
I don't see all of his face,
just flashes as he sits down.

Even in a Free Clinic, I'd say,
technology trumps tenderness
as Dr. Apple goes on typing.

Eye contact? Hello?
He has a hectic day, I know,
not one second to look up.

I am here to "be seen"
for my bum knee, only that,
but he only sees his screen.

I watch his tasseled shoes.
The man has feet, he's human;
maybe he also has a heart.

He has fingers; they move.
I snag a glimpse of his gold ring.
Did he wed a Samsung or a Dell?

After two brief questions,
more tap-tap on his computer,
he exits, on to his next case.

I take off my paper gown.
What if I ran naked in the hall?
I'd be screened out by a screen.

To Dr. Apple, I'm a throwaway
just a blip on his landscape.
I'm relieved as I escape it.

Tell Me the Truth

Am I crazy or is it the world?
Sometimes it's hard to know.

On the steps of a city church
I watch from a still summit,
looking sane, which I am,
maybe serene, even sedate.
I have no cart, only one bag.
I don't appear to be homeless
like many others of my "kind."

I watch a man grating beets
at a jammed intersection.
Crouching on the gray curb,
he's demonstrating his tools.
Crowds step over the man
as they rush toward a bus.
A cyclist downs the grater.
No one stops, no one looks.
Rising, he grabs a new beet.

I'm used to this city's rush;
it's not at all startling to me.
I have lived on these streets.
I can't pity the commuters,
the cyclist, the beet grater,
though they might pity me
if they knew my role in life.
None of it makes any sense;
why should it, what does?

I just want to be answered.
Am I crazy or is it the world?

Noon Musings: We Still Laugh

Why should laughter be invisible?

You can't look into its eyes
or book it for a cruise
though you can take it to dinner.

That does not seem honor enough
for something that heals, tickles,
tells of mirth and gives it back.

Its sister, joy, is equally invisible,
but we can see their linked effects,
like the signs of blowing wind.

How would laughter really look
if it were to appear, corporeal,
before us and among us all?

Sun's lilting glints on ocean waves?
The hip-hop dance of a purple kangaroo?
A fountain speaking French in your backyard?

The sound of three knees knocking?
A dachshund as a tango partner?
All or none of the above?

Beyond the front door of this house,
thought to be a home of misery,
I hear laughter's sparkle,
best when shared as it is here.

Laughter is contagious, universal, unexplained,
leaving us but not quite leaving us alone.

Maybe it remains as it is by precise design.

It can't be trapped, displayed or analyzed
and no one holds its copyright.
Laughter, certainly unseen as air,
music, hope or love,
is free to anyone
everywhere.
at once.

Afternoon Musings: Chatter

Around the planet everyone's talking.
Even where night darkens the earth
numberless people talk in their sleep
while others go on conversing by day.

Countless words fly through the air,
all at one time, all in one moment,
like a vast migration of birds in flight,
wings spread out, beating the wind.

Imagine words had color and form,
dimensions unseen ever before —
the sky would fill with bright confetti,
rising, crossing, speeding, spinning.

Collisions would be inevitable —
unless there were traffic controllers,
prescribed limitations and navigation,
learned from the stars in their courses.

But disputes would be quick to develop:
Are some words more vital than others?
Should long words outstrip the small?
Perhaps all words are created equal?

Let us hope that words remain unseen
or they might blot out the sun and moon,
creating more complications to manage.
But this crisis is already in the making.

Night Musings: Quiet

At first, I can't remember how it comes,
falling like the shade of an umbrella
opened over bathers on a beach.

I am more attuned to jagged lines of
eruptions, disruptions, interruptions
cutting through the nervous air.

Quiet is a country I revisit when I can,
following the ancient trails within;
I, a pilgrim, breaching borders.

I know I'm there when my pace slows,
the temperature around me drops.
Abruptly, then, I know my way.

The signposts, all invisible, appear:
This is a way and that is a way,
meandering, illogical but right.

Here is the braided quiet of friends,
together without needing to speak;
honoring space between words.

There is the quiet carried by music,
by a weaver at her clacking loom,
by a painter, his brush in midair.

And that aroma of freshly cut grass,
the scent from a single teacup,
one juiced squeeze of a lemon.

Always, I sink into echoing quiet
at my remembered cathedral;
its candles' dance, bluish light.

It is in two lovers' naked embrace;
on a bus, in a face, you find it;
a weary face, patient, worn.

Hear the leaves fall in October.
Hear the dark falling each night.
Hear words falling from a book.

Hear me? Are you listening?
Hello? Is anybody out there?
I'll ask again: Who's listening?

THREE

Night Timing

sky's fire dies
sun a closing eye
trees burn out
leaving ash

night a membrane
pinned in place
by small tacks
of kazillion lights

weak sound rising
first a whimper
then a baby's cry
intense insistent

lifted siren's voice
streaking hot red
slashes darkness
then melts away

morning listens
for its first cue
insomniacs await
dawn's entrance

curtain going up
earth applauding
sun an open eye
the sleepless sleep

night's membrane
losing its place
falling faster now
its time expires as

each
pin
drops
out

A Circle

My life is a circle drawn with a stick,
sharp as a quill pen inscribing each year
in a pattern as free as it is strict.
The shape was ignored, perhaps from fear,
but I study the pattern closely now
as the circle begins its last turnings.
The centrifugal force guiding the pace
seems nearer; or am I more discerning?

I never moved in predictable lines,
ever surprised as I followed the curves,
not conscious of any larger design,
though I envy linear lives I observe.
Earth's ancient circles hallow our time,
a gift in itself, not earned or deserved.

Our varied lives are more than simple mime,
they are the handprints we will leave behind.

Inner Landscapes

Is yours one of those green places,
perhaps a grassy stretch of meadow,
freckled with wild flowers, mainly poppies,
and sheep, creamy as autumn clouds,
pausing as a distant church bell chimes?

If so I envy and resent you but never mind.

Or is yours a broad and open space,
layered with tan and bronze and copper;
a sun-kissed desert, open to the sky,
with stately rocks, remote, eternal,
and expensive beamed glass houses?

If so I don't understand but be at peace.

Maybe yours is a wooded mountainside,
a dense mint, hiding bears and bobcats,
where sudden hailstorms damage roofs
and roads are glossy death in wintertime,
though you get those color postcard views.

If so I neither envy nor resent you so enjoy.

Your life could be a small Midwestern town
or a suburb or a tenement or a riverside.
Wherever that may be, it has molded us.
I never had a sense of home and place,
and I have suffered for that, I believe.

I am not the cityscape where I grew up;
its sun-tipped marble roofs don't lure me.
Nor am I that sandy childhood seaside
nor even a blue-eyed New England lake.
Now, homeless, I remain on home's trail.

So do not envy or resent me as I search.

Aging As We Feast

If life turns out to be a formal banquet,
clearly I have finished my main course.
A waiter whisked my dinner plate away,
then scraped crumbs off the tablecloth.
What's left? Sweets, coffee, liqueurs:
three signs of the nearing shut-down.
But please, don't rush us out too fast;
let us linger over the last of the wine.

If life, instead, is actually fast food fare.
— which seems to me a lot more likely —
maybe fries, a burger, a large Coke —
I've already emptied my containers.
Ahead is only three tough cookies
as I move toward the final window.
But please, don't rush us out too soon.
Let us savor our drinks for a while.

If life happens to be a stand-up deal
on a city street beside a vendor's cart,
I've had the hot dog, mustard, bun,
even the pretzel and the indigestion.
Now I await a vanilla ice cream cup;
no chestnuts — they're out of season.
But please don't hurry me away now;
It all goes by so quickly, do not rush.

Now life may be a donut in a Dumpster,
a soup kitchen's random veggie stew
where you get an apple or an orange.
I'll eat mine later with my buddies.
Oh how that orange spray does rise,
like an act of God, new every time.
So let us sit and savor that splash.
Wait. Don't hustle us into the dark.

Lunch Table at the Shelter

In my silence I tell stories.
No one hears them now
amid the chattering of cups,
the arguments of plates,
the complaints of glasses
as we finish our Kool-Aid.

The women request a tale:
our own tradition after lunch.
I, the shelter's only storyteller,
must duck out of my silence.
I tell the one about the woman
on a long road with her friends.

She vows to shorten the road.
No one believes she's able.
So the women tells a story,
then another, then two more.
The long road ends quickly;
it was shortened by the tales.

The women nod their heads;
The dim place has brightened
as if a yellow window opened
in the dining room's gray walls.
Outside there is rain and fog
but not inside this shelter.

There, for maybe half an hour,
every woman at that shaky table
felt a thing she could not name;
it was so strange, so unfamiliar.
Finally, they got it, all at once.
They felt they were at home.

Wandering in the Art Museum

This is where I want to live forever.

Lock me into this pale palace,
leave me overnight, forget I'm here,
I'll hide behind an old exhibit's screens.

I want to look with these painters' eyes
into the windowed worlds they saw,
never found by anyone before or since.

I want to be an angel's wing brushing
layers upon layers of new colors,
captured inside rectangles and squares.

Still as a fresh fall of heavy snow,
pulsing as a red transplanted heart,
this place fuses all its contradictions.

I hear my footsteps echo in the hall
where I walk alone but not alone
because I move past so many figures.

I stop at Van Gogh's famed painting,
The Starry Night, the work of a sad man,
homeless, crazed at times, as he created

stars as they had never spangled skies before
until this misfit, this madman, changed them
for all of us who meet him here at last.

I move on, noticing two feet beneath a screen.
That must be Lil, my friend who visits the museum
in the afternoons since she lost another job.

Many homeless people find a way to wander here,
or sit down on a leather bench, a luxury for us,
where the paintings welcome us with silent speech.

Yes. Let me live here for an hour or a lifetime
where the misfits are accepted and their paintings
hang with the assurance they are housed.

Light along the Way

In a room titled "The Lounge,"
beyond the no-color sofas,
beyond the lamps, askew,
beyond the crippled card table
beyond the TV, chained,
rose a striking line of figures
on a yellow plasterboard wall.

These were life-sized portraits
of selected heroines from history,
painted by a resident of this house,
a women's shelter for the homeless.
Side by side, shoulder to shoulder,
the artist's choices seemed to leap,
rendered in brilliant poster paints:

Rosa Parks with Susan B. Anthony,
Queen Elizabeth and Billie Holiday,
Eleanor Roosevelt by Annie Oakley,
Harriet Tubman with her North star,
Maya Angelou and Jackie Kennedy,
a growing list, reaching high and far;
every week a new figure appeared.

I sat watching the mural as a guest
in that rough shelter on the afternoon
this work was changed in an odd way:
two women fell against Miss Anthony;
a full-length crack marred Susan B,
throwing all the figures out of line.
I knew repair was an unlikely dream.

The artist took a long look at the wall.
For a while she smoked in silence.
When she turned to me, she smiled.
"I think I like it better just this way,"
she squinted, stood back, nodded.
I wondered if she really meant that.
"Seems like us," she said, finally.

Taking the Collection

Church is the only place
    where I find my moorings.
That's been the way of it for me,
    until my moorings snapped.

Sitting in the last pew,
    I knew I was home again.
I left a nickel in the basket
    when they took Collection.

Never had I dared do that,
    I didn't want attention.
That day I felt connected;
    I gave all I could afford.

I could hear the ushers
    behind me in the entry.
They had paper money,
    but the nickel irked them.

The total would not
    be a rounded number.
I listened, shameless,
    to the stew over my offering.

Don't count the nickel;
    That was their solution.
Suddenly I was on my feet.
    I strode into the entry.

"That nickel is mine,"
    I glared at every face.
"The widow's mite," I snapped.
    "You've never heard of it?"

There was a silence.
    Moving to the doors,
I looked at the men
    and I slammed out.

I go to other churches now.
    The ushers cannot rob me.
I will not give up my mooring
    or think of *them* as God.

I still worship; I pray.
    I give all I am to Him,
but since that Sunday
    — I don't give a dime.

That Woman with the Knife

"Who the hell runs the place? I need a signature."
This United Parcel man has not been here before;
his face is red as rare roast beef; I remember well.

This is a house of women, maybe that unnerves him.
He may think we're prostitutes, it often happens.

"That woman with the knife," funny Lil advises him.
A shadow of fear falls across his face, amusing us all.
I look around at the crowd gathered here at lunchtime.

How can we appear so terrifying to so many now?
"That woman with the knife," Lil teases the man.

Sister Nan is slicing a donated loaf of homemade bread.
She wears no habit, just her usual jeans and denim shirt.
Tall, slender, blonde-gray, she seems to shock this man.

With the knife in her left hand, she signs for the delivery.
The UPS man stares. "You're no Sister," he blurts out.

"Not yours, anyway," she tells him, returning to the bread.
We never saw a man escape from her, from us, so quickly.
Laughter rises among us but Sister Nan stops it cold.

"Not funny," she says. "For many reasons. So. Let's eat."
Lil bends her dark head as she says the Blessing for us.

Sister Nan is tough, smart, and soft at her center.
"That man," she says now, "We made him feel bad."
We all protest — he made us feel like circus freaks.

"So who's right?" Nan's Brooklyn accent has a punch.
"No one. Everyone. " Lil says finally, "That's how it is."

"Are there answers anymore, just a Yes or a No?" I ask.
"I don't think so, college girl," Lil waves her knife at me.
I laugh, I'm used to those usual affectionate tweaks.

"Right or wrong, I don't give a shit," Lil laughs now.
"I just want to eat my goddamn grilled cheese in peace."

Men

I think of them as tall trees
I no longer want to climb.
A big one fell on top of me
and fractured me in two
in threes and seventeens.

It took me so long to mend
I never tried to climb again.
Straight pines, red maples
oaks and elms and birch —
they don't even tempt me.

Life has grown far simpler.
My own care and feeding
is enough for me to handle.
I won't take on those risks
that go with climbing trees,

unless a canopy of shelter,
attached to a strong trunk,
happens to appear for me.
What's the chance of *that?*
I don't believe in fairy tales.

Do you really think I should?

Friend

Lil's eyes brim with night
moonless her gaze
even in morning's light.
Every day of the week
she walks beside me
into the sun-struck street
where she likes to sing.

*"The old gray mare, she
ain't what she used to be,"*
in her bluesy bass voice,
always on-key, on-pitch,
but never loud, never that:
"They'll think I'm crazy,"
she often reminds me.
"They already do," I say.

Night in her eyes again.
I should shut up, I think.
But after a few more steps,
she hums *Swanee River,*
a favorite tune, a good sign.
Lil Ryan sang the blues
in several cocktail lounges
in her other life, as we say,
never giving or asking details.

They stalk us, our past lives.
We don't look back at them.
Keep walking, walk faster,
quick now, turn that corner,
cross that gridlocked street
and we'll lose the tall stalker,
at least for an hour a day.
"Hello Dolly, well Hello..."
Night is still in Lil's eyes.

Lil's Question

"If you left," I say, "You would be
the white wing of an angel,
not a woman's black eye."

Lil asks, "What if I did leave?
"What if I made the break now
instead of waiting for Easter?

"Could I make a clean cut,
never see him one more time,
instead of waiting for Christmas?

"Should I do it now, no goodbyes,
go off while he's at that bar,
instead of waiting for whatever?

"Ain't getting no younger, nope,
time won't wait around for me,
I mean that's for goddam sure.

"He'd never come after me, right?
Forget me flat, sure he will, sure,
and I don't owe that man nothing.

"Me, I'd love to be an angel's wing,"
Lil says, finally. "Me, a wing, yeah.
Not just a shiner on some woman."

Let Me Tell Her

Imagine you could peel yourself
off that old charred ruin of a wall.
Rinse the darkness from your soul
until you look like nude spaghetti.

Imagine you can choose new colors
from a tray that holds the spectrum.
If you think this is a childish game
play anyway; what have you to lose?

Imagine wearing purple dusk to bed.
Consider the gold of cats' eyes or
shades of butter, blood, and brandy.
Offer no commitments, there is more.

Imagine fingering that tray. Explore.
Finally, select what won't wash out.
Don't go wild with DayGlo orange,
pick what looks like your best day.

Imagine your time is limited for this
or the tray will leave you with gray.
Choose well but remember this:
Stay away from charred dark walls.

Imagine you can stop imagining
and do, act, be your chosen color.
If you don't believe in changing,
I'll believe for you until you do.

Omens

on the roof's peak
three blue-black crows
one behind another
their inked wings unfurled
one after another
looking like a single bird
one before another
moving as a single bird
one backing another
like a 'fifties girl group
one miming another
like Angels of Death
staying by the others
Death in triplicate above
waiting with the others
but for what, for whom?
Cawing to each other
as the trash truck arrives.
Other omens?
I don't know.
Yet.

Where Lil Went

No one knows. No one's seen her, not today.
She's a longtime regular for lunch here at Gilead.
Sister Nan calls around to the other shelters.
No sign of Lil, not even at the museum, nowhere.

Just after lunch, I shortcut to the public library
and trip over Lil, dead and cold, in a back alley,
her throat's red slash, the empty open eyes
— they make me turn to vomit in a trash can.

Then I lean over her and weep, wetting her face.
She's stiff, her fingers claws, nails just done.
I've seen murdered girls before; it doesn't help.
I walk back to Gilead. The women read my face.

There's nobody to identify the body except us.
There's no one who can lay Lil out; only us.
Sister Nan finds a priest and we light candles.
Flowers appear. Prayers are said. We cry.

The burial is at some far-off field for "Indigents."
Only Sister Nan can go; returning, she is ashen.
We can't find a spare white sheet or black crepe.
We drape Lil's chair in a red Mexican tablecloth.

Missing Her

Her wide mouth
encircling a scream
left to stiffen that way

arms flung out wide
crucified to midnight
legs spread apart

for her invaders entry
all borders breached
men piling on/in her

to shut the bitch up
they would think
one slashing blade

her death-wound
a bold red gash
open as her lips

come back to me
my fondest friend
don't abandon me

somehow return
we'll laugh again
if I only knew how

Grief

It fills me as rainwater fills a spout.
It fills me as an apple fills its skin.
It fills me as earth fills in a grave.

When will it spill, split, settle down?
These things take time, so I'm told.
I shout, "To hell with lines like that."

Everyone at lunch is staring at me.
"I've had my fill of filling up with pain,"
I hiss the words in a furious whisper.

"To hell with making life look pretty,"
I turn. "I could bake a cake, I guess,
iced and decorated with Lil's name."

Sister Nan speaks quietly to me:
"Lil's death hurts us all, not just you."
I know that but my anger still boils.

Later, trudging off to the night shelter,
I see my rage bloom like a red rose
growing big enough to swallow me.

In the center of this rose sits our Lil,
looking well, unharmed, but frowning.
"Live, damn it, you owe that to me."

I've heard this earlier in my dreams.
"And who else do I owe?" I demand.
"You know." She says. "Yourself."

The rose of rage appears to shrink.
I spatter the sidewalk with my tears.
Ashamed, I'm reaching out for Lil.

She's fading away into a faded rose.
"*Yourself,* girl." She disappears.
"Come back," I call but she is gone.

On the street, people stare at me.
I wipe my wet face and trudge on,
knowing now what I have to do.

"Damn," I hiss at the heavens.
It's hard to have so many debts.
Even harder, paying them off.

I see my anger rising up again:
this time, only a streak of red.
"Okay," I shout. "I promise."

The red streak is wavering
before it fades to violet,
then into a creased blue.

That Other Place

a house bearded in ash
dust abruptly silver-
struck by fingers
of fading sun
gapped floorboards
dropping shafts
attic to cellar
half-hinged doors
hanging at a slant
window panes
a webbed maze
of cracks and
crazed patterns
like hoarfrost
walls with squares
of nothingness
where photos hung
the crooked gate
a kitchen plate
left on the steps
for a lost cat
and wind in
the chimney
always keening
sighing saying
"Here I lived
when I'm in
depression."

The Journey

Take care when you turn inward.
Only miners understand the risk.

You find a seam within your mind.
There, beneath a covering, lies ore.

When a tunnel leads into a shaft
you enter the steep darkness alone.

Your past mistakes will then appear,
tugging at you, scolding in unison.

Do not hold any debates with them;
at that level they will always win.

Brush past this swarm, go deeper,
but remember to climb up and out.

Visit but don't camp among your sins.
Surface fast with all you've learned.

You live to die and die to many lives:
but do not mistake Death for a lover.

If your brain begins to list last words,
note each one but file the best away.

I chant this litany to myself as prayer.
Survival is your job, I say: *Begin again.*

Where Am I Now?

Where you go matters less than going.
Where you've been is a skein of days.
Plant your seeds and watch them growing;
if you don't know how, do it anyway.

As our fragile lifetimes seem to shorten,
old questions turns urgent and pressing.
We may feel lost while we shift gears;
as we go on we burn for a blessing.

Friends die, jobs end; we ask ourselves
why we survive at times of change.
We're called to probe, to explore, to delve
into crannies we must now rearrange.

How can we fill the new space in our lives?
We want to furnish it with what matters,
what lasts, what contributes, what thrives;
strong thread to mend tears and tatters.

Where to begin spinning cloth into gold?
How to learn such an art? Hard to say.
Collect and gather up all that you hold,
then use it, share it, and give it away.

Break-In At Gilead

They came in through the roof's hatch
on a Wednesday morning at five-thirty
no one there to stop them on the stairs
later the police said it was three of them
running down the shelter's creaky steps
through the hall and past the "front parlor"
where we often sat to gossip after lunch
knocking over chairs in the dining room
furious by then that we had no TV to take
no radio not even any stashed computers
on into the kitchen I'd mopped Tuesday
where they hit our enormous freezer to
steal our eleven homemade casseroles
then the cans stored in the cupboards
bread and forty packages of Kool-Aid
leaving only the milk before they ran off
with all our food stowed in several bags
so when the staff and volunteers arrived
the fridge and doors and drawers were
open wide and empty except for crumbs
shocking us into a large dark silence
closing in on us like a room's four walls
and only then did I see our Sister weep.

Arthur's Surprise

Mondays we got brownies with lunch
after days of canned mixed fruit.

Arthur was a string bean of a man,
a shy one, he never talked to us.

Solemn as a priest, he brought his gift,
then darted to his dental office.

When he first came to Gilead, he said:
"Arthur, you finally did it. *Yes.*"

For years, his brownies arrived.
He didn't speak but gave us a grin.

When the brownies didn't come
We saw him in the obituaries.

We grieved for him, not his gifts.
His ashes were sent home to Iowa.

I think about him still, this shy man
who did something that mattered.

Some small thing that took all
his courage, his nerve and his daring.

Maybe we gave something to him,
we the poor, the homeless; Nobodies.

I'll never know but that's my guess.
Here's to you, Arthur: *You did it — yes.*

FOUR

Social Worker's Update, 1990

Andromeda Lane
AKA "Andie"

Age: 39 yrs old

Family situation: Unchanged

Issues:
Trauma at 19
Possible sexual abuse
Relives it but highly functional

Work Situation:
Held four jobs
Accident 1988
Strong leadership at Gilead
Edits shelter newsletter
Takes on many shelter chores

Psych Eval:
Normal, good
Tested well

Ready for Transitional Housing
More than ready, actually
None available at this time

Prognosis:
Continues positive
Could live on her own
Finances an issue

The Big Question

What kind of craziness keeps us going?
We, the hapless hopeless homeless,
why don't we lie down, give up?

I wonder — then I think it out.

What kind of craziness keeps men
climbing up Mount Everest,
despite the cold, the risk?

What kind of craziness keeps artists
at their paints and canvasses,
when no one buys their work?

Spurned lovers go on loving — why?

We all hope to reach that peak,
sell the paintings,
win the love,
start again.

Is it craziness to see life as God's gift,
not a tee-shirt you return,
haggling for a discount?

There are no discounts in this life,
I learned that pretty fast.

And none of this is craziness, I say.
I call it sanity and nothing more.
I call it grit and nothing less.

Lulu's Good Night

"Try a graveyard for sleeping,
the right one, the right spot,
where you lay out your bedroll
on a dry tombstone, kept up,
and girl, you made your bed.

"I liked the hilltop cemetery,
cut grass, them swept paths
a place got itself cut grass,
you know what I'm saying.
Private, for us, what a kick.

"Nothing, trust me, moved
inside that big old open fence
No one come there at night
where that big old sky, it
blends in nice with trees.

"Not a sound to tap your ears
except the leaves whispering
like they have their language
you just don't comprehend but,
trust me, sometimes they sing.

"I slept under them marble wings
of a angel carved at my head.
Well, I swear, she was shelter;
them big wings kept off the rains
go on, laugh, that's God's truth.

"It ended for me at the graveyard
when two horny teenaged kids
made the next tombstone a bed,
the two of them stripped down,
woo-hoo, they was hot, uh-huh.

"My Lord, the noises they made,
who could carry on the loudest,
who could groan the longest,
who could sound the wildest —
like a damn orgasm contest.

"Maybe they figured I was dead.
Likely they never saw me at all.
Well, I saw the last of them both
after three nights and one hour
when I took myself to this shelter."

So spoke my friend, Lulu White,
who, as it happened, was black,
and a fine lady, that she was, too.
She made us laugh, tough to do,
on the chapel shelter's cold floor.

Regal, tall, graceful, Lulu was our
"African Queen," a title she liked.
Her hair salon had burned down;
flat broke, she was still royalty,
an elegant, ebony icon among us.

Awake at Night

In the window a blood-moon hangs
looking like a small child's red balloon,
merry, shy, and joyous on its unseen string.

I watch it from my mattress at the shelter,
sorry that the sleeping women around me
can't look up to catch this passing sight.

We quarrel here at times, as all families do,
but one small wonder heals most cracks;
awe and fear unite the "regulars" like me.

I hear the sighs and snores and whimpers
of the women sleeping on this chapel floor;
though I lie among them, I know I'm alone.

To have a red moon-balloon all to myself
should make me feel honored, privileged,
grateful, and so I am, but I am still alone.

Understand, I don't feel sorry for myself,
but reality sometimes slaps you in the face
and you remember what you try to forget.

I'll tap a memory of ice-cream sundaes:
vanilla hills dripping with hot fudge sauce,
always with red cherries on their peaks.

I dreamed about those cherries as a child.
Perhaps I'll dream about them as a woman,
while that red globe looks in to remind me.

Sleep

I tell you now
don't waste your sleep
dream yourself out of here
speed your spirit away

Dream
A man with a violin
stands under your window
playing a fast polka
in the faint morning light
his eyes bright as dimes
asking you to dance

Dream
A woman in your kitchen
turning potatoes into roses
on a garden-green table
her beet-stained fingers
beckoning you

Dream
yourself into a cottage
with flamingo pink walls
like the deep rose chair
where a white cat
is waiting for you

Dream
where you want to go
and you'll be there
a moment, an instant
forgetting you sleep
on a shelter's floor

Dye Job

My hair is greenish blonde now,
due to Lulu's onetime salon pals;
they gave bottled dye to her
for practice on those willing.

The color washes out, she swears.
Meanwhile I look pretty funky,
like those dolls who mimic trolls;
I laugh at random mirrors.

This afternoon I'll be shampooed
back to my old graying auburn
but you never know with Lulu,
I might next be aqua blue.

"Gonna get this right," she says.
"Gonna get back to Beauty School,
get me a job, get the hell out."
I hope she will this time, I do.

But when she spirals downward
from a giddy, giggly manic high,
depression waits: an open grave
ready for her fall down and in.

Then she rises from the earth,
maybe a month later or less,
to ride a tide of newborn wind,
flying high over our heads.

Life is ups and downs for her
if she doesn't take her meds
but who can tell her this?
For now I wear her blue.

Memories Are Life

I have a few
as we all do
housed or homeless
they live in us
I see two faces
so often I forget
how many times
I summon these
who need no
summoning at all
they wait within
already there
a breath away.
Both peasants,
working women,
Irish and Romani,
they save my life
so often I wonder
if I weary them —
but not them, no.
I want to ask
everyone I meet:
who waits within,
eternally, for you?

My Survival Trainer

Ageless as earth, stronger than pain,
her eyes the blue that centers a flame,
she held our troubled home together,
sustaining all of its malignant elegance
by the ligaments and tendons of her will.

She filled cracks in our papered walls,
spackled holes created by hurled plates,
smoothed deep creases out of wrinkled air
with her rough big-knuckled peasant hands,
so I'd "grow up straight," is how she put it.

As she plunged her long-handled brushes
into the depths of toilet bowls and drains,
she gave voice to Irish songs, often this:
I wish I was in Carrickfergus....I bet she did.
She raised me on tales, spuds, tough loving.

Was it the stories, songs, or simply herself
that cleared our home's acidic atmosphere?
Did her powerful presence absorb our ills,
scrub off domestic warfare, if only for a day?
Send grudges and rage out of the windows?

Any ailing section of the house was treated
with a feather duster, soft old cloths, wax,
sometimes with spit, real spit, and polish.
Glass was shined with old newspapers;
the home, lemon-scented, shifted its weight.

If there was anger in the master bedroom,
she took me to her room; I slept in her bed.
She taught me how to become a survivor.
Though she, an immigrant, felt homeless,
she herself was my house — my home.

I Reach Back For Her

She was the row of buttons fastening my dress,
the stream of raw honey on a kitchen spoon.
She was the star-pricked sky of August nights,
and the click-click-click of blue Rosary beads.
She was the knife carving a pear's unbroken peel
and the stern face of the woman in the moon.

I was the whining child sleeping in her narrow bed
and the girl who sat under the altar in church.
I was her assistant as she went about her chores,
and the rapt audience for her magical stories.
I was the infant she baptized in the kitchen's sink
and the kid who settled flowers in Holy Water.

She was an exiled Irish peasant, she claimed;
was I the one who must be an exile like her?
Was she my nanny or my secret mother —
a subject not touched, revealed, discussed?
Was she in my mind because she loved me
or was I a growing branch of her strong tree?

You owe it to me, she says, in my deepest dreams
to break the cycle and be who you are.
You can't remain an exile, she says,
stop this wheel from forever turning.

Roma Grandmother

In a line of painted wagons you
were born. "On roads," you said,
"We lived, we died." A "Gypsy"
Compania was your first tribe.
There you did and did not thrive.

At fourteen you ran into the dark,
leaving kin and that old man you
must wed — to Bucharest you fled
alone, never allowed to go home.

You sewed to pay your passage
sailing with a shawl and an icon.
You, frail as forsythia, firm as fists,
took your icon through Ellis Island.

Old when I was young, you were
doll-like and diamond-hard
smelling of paprika and peaches
you sewed my father's "breeches."

Now I face aging and think of you;
I am ashamed to admit what's true:
You journeyed into the Unknown
and I fear traveling to God alone.

Ancestors

How brave they were, the great-grandparents,
stepping out into their new landscape,
streets unpaved with promised gold.

How gingerly they moved, the great-grandparents.
carrying a Rosary, paired candlesticks,
housed and roofed only by their shawls.

How little they brought in, the great-grandparents,
something old, maybe blue, nothing new
except for the terrain spreading ahead.

How hopefully they walked, the great-grandparents,
refusing to throw one backward glance,
they bore within them seeds of children.

How quick their pace became, the great-grandparents,
climbing up five fights of narrow stairs
to one-room flats, their low-rent homes.

How quickly they settled in, the great-grandparents,
sharing toilets, tables, skillets, sheets,
mindful of the coming generations.

How forgetful we can be, the great-grandchildren,
sleeping on the streets they paved for us,
or fighting over our mats in a shelter.

Bedroom Ceiling

It is what I remember most about that room

where I dreamed of lost boyfriends, lost dogs
and red-hot horses charging in a tented circle.

My eyes would open on that ceiling, aging then,

like an elevated dance floor, facing downward,
scuffed but useful, waiting for one final tango.

How many daylight hours did I waste there,

pinned to the bed with migraines or depression,
staring at the patient ceiling, always waiting?

I wished I could fold it up like a great blanket

or a quilt pieced by some long-forgotten hands
so I could take it with me, folded in my bags.

But this ceiling reappears wherever I am,

projecting itself on unexpected surfaces,
a canopy for me and all my old red horses.

Its cracks formed a design like some odd face

I'd always known but couldn't place or name.
Now it winks, grinning; it has come with me.

Still Life with Giraffes

They came here as a peddler's gift
of painted clay and braided grass.

Paired now they stand tall but shy
on a table, donated, made of glass.

In our dim and shabby city shelter,
the giraffes look festive but aghast.

Near them, a wooden tray holds
grapes, their prime clearly past.

But this still-life can delight the eye,
even the these out-of-place giraffes.

They were painted red, blue, yellow,
colors that can laugh and leap and last.

A window frames this combination,
merry, international and unsurpassed

as a marriage of artistry and poverty,
it's a hit here, as a symbol, unsurpassed.

We know its hopefulness can't fix our world;
but we see it as a sign, an omen, a forecast.

The Hive

I'm never afraid to go into the hive:
that is the public library downtown.
The moment I go in I hear its buzz:
Like bees, hidden but always present,
were all those syllables moving together
— humming as they turn into words,
swarming, small and black, into books.

Within that honeycomb, there in the hive,
I am no longer homeless, no longer alone.
It's always like that for me in such places.
In my old life, I loved the college library;
at night, as it closed and I left for my dorm,
I'd look back at the soaring stone walls
enclosing the shelves, enveloping books.

Now, in my new life, there is a new hive.
There I go, two afternoons a week or so,
after lunch and hanging out at Gilead,
where I like to help clean up the kitchen.
Three friends came with me, only in winter,
for warmth in a place that would accept us.
Always there for me, the shabby, dusty hive.

Cracks

Like veins in a hand,
like creases in brows,
like lines in pursed lips,
this street's crazy cracks
tell their unspoken stories.

Cares were borne here,
as trucks trundle loads
over bridges' steel spans
and barges haul cargo
across cities' main rivers,
their skin graying now
but determined to flow.

Hopes quickened here,
the fragrance of promise
still smells like cut grass,
still maps destinations
for the bold and the brisk
with somewhere to go,
meet, deal, dine, tick-tock.

Rage was stamped here,
steps slamming like doors,
fury driving paired feet,
but despair left a shuffle,
a slow sinking into cement,
inking the pavement black:
what was the point anyway?

But children still dance here,
crowing as they take a leap,
zigzagging with the cracks,
reveling in their patterns,
freeform, irreverent, illogical,
yet in their eccentric paths,
holy as a cathedral's maze.

Fighting Mad

Sue, a regular like us, was off her meds;
we knew it when she took the hammer.

On Gilead's top floor we heard it first:
Sue shut and smashed every window.

She worked her way to the second floor;
we heard the crash of shattering glass.

Slowly we moved close to one another,
even those with grudges, even spite.

Some of us recalled this other Susan
with that crazy laser light in her blue eyes.

Now we heard her feet stomp the stairs.
Useless, dialing 911, they rarely came.

The footfalls stomped louder, nearer;
glass was falling down into the street.

Sue, we called out, *Susan, Susan, Sue,*
we called, keened, wailed, whimpered,

as if her name was some magic word,
a spell, a blessing, that could stop her.

Suddenly, she was there staring at us,
her fair hair wild, eyes lit, hammer raised.

We cringed like some frightened kids,
winced as one and no body was speaking.

Slowly, Sue lifted up a folding chair.
Raised it. Threw it. Watched it. Waited.

The air split into flying fragments as it fell;
for me, for us, time stalled and stopped.

Only Sister Nan moved in the quiet,
inching toward the woman with the hammer.

Sue didn't see the nun sneak behind her
and then Nan was on Sue's back,

climbing it like a tree, shinnying up its trunk,
until she had reached Sue's shoulders.

Grabbing an arm, then a wrist, then a hand,
Nan struggled to capture the hammer.

A demon's roar rose from Sue's throat,
so loud the house seemed to tremble.

Writhing, she tried to shake the nun off
but Nan rode the wave called Susan.

All at once the hammer slammed the floor
as it fell and Sue fell on her face in tears.

* * *

A year later, it was my turn to serve lunch,
At table number two Sue sat down to eat.

I set a plate of before her: spaghetti, I think.
Then the Kool-Aid, then a fork; a spoon.

No eerie light in those blue eyes now;
I saw the medicine bottles on the table.

"Looking good," I said. "Yep," she smiled.
"Why'd y'all get these new windows?"

Tiny Blue Chair

I ran from you when the madness began
and your face wasn't yours anymore
and you yelled "Go to Hell" on the street.

yours was the face I had always wanted
to see in my mirror one day some day
when I wasn't eleven years old anymore.

yours was a dense emerald gaze
like a medieval maze that drew me
in until I thought I'd found the center.

no one else had an aunt who was Paris
and perfume — and that oddity, in 1958,
power with an office and a briefcase.

you could hold fire in the quick flash of
your cigarette lighter and you drank
Scotch neat, like a man, I thought.

in church I watched your etched profile
veiled by the tremulous membrane
of your lace mantilla and you smiled.

you only wept on Good Friday when
we made the Stations together but
then you began weeping at mass,

at street corners and cash registers
and near a gutter on Fifth Avenue
where you threw your wedding ring.

frightened, I ran for help but I didn't
think help would be the hospital,
the psych ward with no way out

breakdowns haunted your family,
I overheard, but I couldn't see
why you went without goodbyes.

I erased your face from my mirror then
afraid I might turn into you as I'd wished
but I did get one package from you:

a tiny beaded wire chair, turquoise blue,
made in group therapy, with a note:
"God's here — please pray anyway."

I never saw you again, despite requests;
what you left to me is simple but your
strong faith and that tiniest blue chair.

Because of you I understand Sue.
You did not know what you gave
to me, to Sue, to Linda, to Lulu.

Magic

It is the genii in the lamp
It is the Yellow Brick Road
It is Juju and Abracadabra
It is medicine, many kinds,
that leads you out of Hell.

So the women say,
most of them, anyway,
those on the magic meds,
prescribed by a doctor,
a god, a wizard, a healer,
who visits our shelter
fortnightly, no charge.

Half of us, maybe more,
live in two different worlds,
one with meals and maps,
however disappointing;
one a marsh of madness,
different for everyone.

I am a one-world girl,
sticking with the map;
many friends are not.
When they hear voices
from their other world,
they may cry in agony;
they may throw shoes.

You have no choice,
the doctor knows this:
Madness is your lot
or it's not, that's a fact.
Doc's magic medicines
throw a calming quilt
over some shoulders;
but magic has a price.

Carla, my new pal,
no longer sees lions
instead of fast cars
as we cross a street
but the meds block
her "angels' voices;"
to her, a deep loss.

Fay hates the meds
for their side effects;
she may quit them,
drift off to the marsh,
then start over again.
Kisha thanks God
for her medicinals:
they banish demons.

We all live together,
psychotic or sane.
accepting who's what.
Our friends in the fog
are not the fog itself;
they're themselves.
On good days, we say,
"Girl, welcome home."

On the Streets

Linda lives inside a blue balloon
no one else can see or even touch.
There she feels safe on the streets
where she watches her shopping cart
filled with all that's left of her last home.

In Linda's blue world there are voices
that have tails trailing like crepe paper,
only softer, longer, sometimes bluer.
They speak a language Linda knows
so she can talk with all the voices.

When she was in a mental hospital
the doctors gave her medications.
Linda was discharged into the city
where she stopped taking her pills.
They kept her from hearing voices.

When I can, I bring her Big Macs;
she trusts me but no one trusts her.
No one, even Linda, knows her story
but she remembers feeling "different,"
teased for that in Manhattan's schools.

Hers is the image of homelessness
most people hold tight in their minds:
the scary toothless hag of nightmare.
Linda doesn't know her many sisters:
sane, unnoticed, blending, fitting in.

For her, night is a jagged black cave,
no entrances, no exits, no daylight.
The stars, lit pinholes in the cave.
The moon, a disapproving silver face.
The only safety is her blue balloon.

When I lived out there on the streets
I sensed danger everywhere and so
I get what Linda means about a cave.
My blue balloons are "real" houses;
Linda's is as real to her as the air.

Nightmare Women

"Look at the bag lady, Mommy,"
the boy with the red balloon points
at my friend Linda and he laughs.
"Don't." His mother jerks him back.
He sticks his tongue out at Linda;
Mom adjusts her designer jeans.
Indignant, I point at both of them.
"Look at that *bagless* lady," I call.
Mother, dragging child, huffs away.
Linda, with her bags, is oblivious.

Instantly, I feel a sharp twist of guilt.
Will we invade that boy's nightmares?
Maybe he has forgotten us already,
maybe not until he shuts his eyes.
Tonight, I'll send my spirit out to him.
I'll say he never saw two witches,
only harmless creatures in disguise
who appeared to him gift-wrapped
by the people who invented iPads.

I'll never know what that kid dreams.
In thirty years, I hope, he'll tell his son
about the night he saw me by his bed,
a figure luminous and pale as pearls,
with a pair of feathered silver wings,
who told him people wear disguises
to conceal their radiance, so bright,
it could hurt or blind your open eyes.

So maybe I can send that spell out
and it will hit its target like a drone.
If people with computers "Skype,"
why can't a homeless woman and
a housed boy connect by thought?
At least when I lie down tonight
in the chapel, I'll hit my mattress
with a mission: dreamwork to do.

My Friend Protests

We weren't born as bag ladies, you know?
I mean, we didn't push carts to kindergarten,
carts full of stuff and crayons and torn clothes.

We weren't born as homeless women, get it?
Our futures weren't sown in our amniotic fluid.
I'm a nurse, I know those words, have for years.

We weren't tramping streets in worn-down shoes
when we were learning algebra, you read me?
We didn't try to spell the word H.O.M.E.L.E.S.S.

We weren't thinking, "Will he hit me in the face?"
when we went to high school dances in the gym
or kissed in the back seat of his car, believe me.

We weren't all destined for street life, understand?
Life screwed our destinies or the other way around.
Sure, some of us chose wrong. Hey, some did *not*.

We weren't crazy in the ninth grade — surprised?
Many of us aren't crazy now, either; I'm quite sane.
Some things happen, not because you screwed up.

We weren't all the same, we're not all the same now.
So often we blend, fit in, work, go home to our cars,
and no one knows who we are, we make sure of that.

You pull away from us like we are contagious.
But we were someone's kid, a girl, a daughter,
same as others. You know what I'm saying now?

Looking into the Future

When I sit in a park,
emptied at dusk,
I can see into the future.
Often I forget it exists.
I see it at moonrise
as light turns the grass
into stiff straight pins.
I see it in my palms,
open to small flickers
from street-lamps lights.

Trees, edged in silver,
speak in their language.
I have no fear there
as long as I remain
in that magical glow.
I take this risk weekly
to catch that reminder:
a future still waits for me:
A different one from now.

That is the silent promise
written by moon-silver
on a splintering bench.
Now that I have dulled
the blur of the wild world,
only then can I read it,
then can I see ahead:
a long yellow avenue,
one large purple house,
a blood-red tree beside
a blue-green woman —
could that woman be me?

Or am I seeing, in a blur,
someone else's future?

To Disappointment

I feel comfortable with you, old friend,
you never/always let me down.

With you I know just what to expect;
I dread Hope's awful suspense.

If I want a relaxing day, I turn to you.
Your record approaches gold.

I feel protective of our close rapport.
If I lost that I'd lose too much.

We have spent most holidays together.
You're on for New Years Eve.

You're there for me and for my friends.
We know we can count on you.

We have quite a history, the two of us.
I look forward to future events.

I'm sure we'll have a lot to talk about.
We're never at a loss for that.

I'll let you know when to let me down.
It won't be long, I'd guess.

I'm one of your best customers, I think,
so save some time for me.

If your let-downs let me down, I'll let go,
but let's not let that worry us.

FIVE

Who's That Behind You?

One behind each chair, they stand around the table,
people from the past whose names we never speak,
but I sense them hovering as we sit down to eat.

Some have sent us on our journeys to this shelter.
Others wonder what happened to take us here.
We can't unknot for anyone our tangled fears.

There is my father who wanted a son, an heir,
and scissored me out of his life after my birth.
And yet, he stands behind me now in grief.

Beside him is my husband who went AWOL
with a case of beer, and most of my savings,
behind him there are only dim engravings.

They are my own mistakes, my wrong turns,
my roads less traveled by, not allowed —
I own them all, I can't deny that crowd.

I am one of many Prodigal Daughters,
too proud, too ashamed for crawling back.
We carry old grudges in our packs.

Consider me among the fortunate.
I wasn't fired, my home did not burn down,
I wasn't left with five kids, no skills, no job.

I'm not astride the sharpened edge of sanity.
I'm well, I don't have that tubercular cough.
I'm not the one who frightened her children off.

Behind them all stand figures from the past,
unable to reach in, fix, solve, edit, scour.
Their valleys may be darker than our own.

All Hallows Eve

Turn out the lights.
All the lights.
Hear the house
lean into the night.
Stir up the fire;
set it spinning
so it trances us
as shadows shift
in each dim corner.
Inch close to me.
Tell us a tale.

Speak of spirits
riding on the wind
then sliding down
to skim our roofs
or watch us from
a glassy window.
Smooth your story
like an old map;
spread it, rustling,
across our knees.

Through this crack
between seasons
two worlds meet:
ours and another.
Ancient wisdom
has reminded us
of more than one.
Departed souls
may be our visitors,
sinners slink in
behind the saints.

What was that?
You heard it, too.
Don't leave me yet.
Shadows weave
webs around us
so we must whisper
about the invisible
as midnight nears.
This is the night
we can see beyond.

City on a Summer Sunday

Dusty trees, brushed with gold,
guard the city's entrance into evening.
We love a cool spell, however deceiving.

An odd quiet falls like displaced snow
over emptied buildings, empty streets;
hives vacated before August's heat.

Above the heft of steel and concrete
low skies dare to hang in softer folds,
old-fashioned veils of violet and rose.

Muted travelers smile but pad away
as if awed by some spirit, some blight
cast upon them by the coming night.

I want to set a lantern on a ledge,
a space no longer than my height.
I'd pour some wine in the magic light.

People wonder why I would dream
of toasting this old depleted turf
and not the beach, the foamy surf?

My reason is not seen easily:
This is when the city gives it to me.

Giving Me a Lift

In this kind of life
you miss kisses,
wools, chocolate,
sure, sometimes,
though I forget now
the taste of a kiss.
Not that it matters.
What I truly crave
is not on that list.
If I tell our women
what I want most,
they tend to laugh,
thinking it's a joke,
but I'll write it here,
one beautiful word:

Apricots. Even one.
I yearn for that fruit,
fresh, never dried,
the velveteen skin
seamless and firm,
enclosing its juice.
The tint of a sunrise,
not peach, not pink,
no a glaring orange,
it is the color of hope.

Is It Time Yet?

Time's a funny thing for us after a while.
The day is forty hours long, maybe more
when it rains and you can't walk outside;
you pace inside, you smoke, you brood.

I've heard that time goes faster as we age
but I say this: it moves the way we move.
When I write in this notebook, let's say,
clock-time stops — or I drop out of time.

Each year I make Christmas ornaments
to sell on streets where I know the cops.
When my fingers twist the reds and greens
I don't give a damn when dinner's ready.

It's the wheeling of the years, most say,
holidays bunching up behind each other,
like people pushing you in subway cars,
that's what gets them, years whizzing by.

They don't whiz by for me or my mates.
There's not much whizzing in our lives.
Days drop like clothes blown off a line
to be gathered, ironed, hung up again.

When I worked the days went faster.
I've served up fries at McDonald's,
waited tables, cycled as a messenger —
until the accident, ending work for me.

I had to go on Public Assistance after that.
Time is slow as I wait for my monthly check
It's like waiting with a number in a bakery
for a slice of chocolate cake you didn't make.

You Never Know When

Fire is a hand from Hell,
always wary, watching, waiting
for the careless hand, the averted eye,
a deep sleeper, birthday candles, leaves.

That sly hand reached
into the front room of our shelter,
grabbed the ancient sofa's fraying edge,
and tried to steal the only "home" we had.

Rainy day, shelter filled:
an ideal time for the fire to strike;
twenty women on line for a hot lunch,
never guessing they could be French Fries.

A ring finger of flame
rose at the far end of the couch,
upholstered as a faded once-grand tapestry,
where the flame's finger grew into a furled fist.

Crowded dining room,
I saw the danger right away,
over the heads and the mostly turned backs;
soon we caught the black bitter stink of smoke.

The fire — first unfurled,
grabbing inches from the couch
before Sister Nan and I could stop it;
now the flames were grabbing still more turf.

Screaming, pushing,
the lines bunched up into one;
women started a stampede as Nan stood,
calling out for calm; no one heard her then.

Shrieks and shoving
as we began to turn into a mob.
Jumping on a table, I lifted my voice:
"Ladies, damn it, *shut up now.*"

A taut silence held.
I shouted, "Grab the parlor rug."
Hands snatched it, raised it, flung it
on the couch and we put that fire out.

A win is rare for us.
No fire ever touched our room.
The only thing to burn that rainy day
was left forgotten in the oven — *lunch.*

Feeling Alive

My feet hurt. My left hipbone hurts.
Holy God, the hair on my head hurts.
I'm not complaining, I'm not whining,
only writing how it is with me just now.

As if I could forget?

Pain is like the paving under our shoes.
It's always there, it's always hardened,
so constant we expect it to be there,
unforgiving gray cement: familiar.

As if we could forget?

Still, pain is more than pavement.
It's a giant web, a net connecting
every living creature on this planet,
shared with trees, men, antelopes.

As if we could forget?

I rarely fight with that communal pain.
It tells me I'm still capable of feeling,
reassures me I'm alive and not alone.
We all share sleep, sound — and pain.

And we do forget.

My Explosion of Rage

Damn it to hell just listen to me

I hate this steep staircase of days
each step I climb each day I climb
I hate them, hear me, hate them

I've had it see had all I can take
all of it and more this is no life
but people think it's my own fault

Not that I'm totally blameless
I made mistakes along the way
well haven't you I bet you have

Oh yes, everybody makes them
but everybody doesn't land here
on these goddamned avenues

This is a life-sentence I hear
once you fall you'll never rise
no parole, no pardon granted.

We all get listless we get tired,
we give in and we just give way
we get numb slack careless but

Get mad — mad as hell
don't let these damn streets
steal your spirit or your soul

Get mad at this life of yours
don't shuffle on and take it
losing your self on the way

Go to Hell you in the suit
you in the dress and heels
you can't get past yourself

So listen to me rant and rage
call it madness call it age
turn away and turn the page

Violets for Valentine's Day

When I see a certain purple
underneath a woman's eye,
I want to reach into her life
and rearrange the furniture.

I'm uninvited, no gate-crasher,
so I reach into my own life,
a grab-bag of bright excuses,
what-ifs, maybes, supposes.

Look at the mess you made,
I scold, which doesn't help.
It stiffens my resistance —
Risk. Change. Try. Shut up.

I'm used to that grab-bag life,
its rags, its junk, its treasures.
Gilead's in-house social worker
wants to take my bag away.

I hate her sincerity, her hair,
a perky bob, her glasses that
magnify her small blue eyes,
twin pins pricking my soul.

For the first time in years
I go into a bar for a drink.
A guy suggests we kiss.
"Valentine's Day," he says.

His groping wet fingers
went down way too far.
I shook him off then —
felt his fist slam my eye.

Later on, I reach the shelter.
Lulu's frantic, horrified.
"Look at you," she hisses.
I lurch into the bathroom.

Both my eyes are bruised.
That purple, here, on me.
"Fool." I spit at the mirror.
"Why?" Lulu, behind me.

"I didn't *cooperate*," I sigh.
Lulu says nothing more.
She knows this story well;
we all do, including me.

Many men never hit us.
That, I know, is also true.
I've chosen ones who do.
No tears now. Try irony.

"Valentine violets," I say.
Lulu, good friend Lulu,
smacks my bottom hard.
I thank her. I needed that.

Nothing is the same again.
I visit the social worker.
Pacing through the night,
half-awake, I hear things.

That maternal Irish voice:
"You owe it to me, girl."
I listen to her voice again.
"You owe it, love, to us."

Seeing in the Dark

The sky is navy-blue at midnight.
low clouds sometimes hide the stars.
In that darkness I can see ahead,
better than I can at garish noon:
our new home awaiting me.

I see it as a series of rectangles
lit and linked to one another,
walls of windows hanging
high above the glimmer of a city
where midnight is also navy-blue.

This home's location is a mystery,
not yet ready to reveal itself
but I sense that it is empty now,
no longer occupied or furnished,
bathing in the night's navy-blue.

My Roma grandmother saw futures,
always in the night, the fluid dark,
and she saw more than I can see:
winning numbers in small lotteries,
deaths, sometimes, in midnight's blues.

The sky hides stars for a good reason,
she told me, *you can't force a vision.*
True, I knew, so I must wait here
for stars to prick a cloudless sky
as my new home must wait for me.

I wonder if my grandmother sees it.
Why ask, you know I do, she says.
At night, will our home show the sky?
Why ask, you know it will, she snaps.
Why else all this midnight navy-blue?

Hand it Over

Whoever has my past hidden away,
Hear this: I'd like to take it back now,
just to edit it, revise, rework, rewrite.

I never got a copyright for my life,
it didn't seem to matter much before.
Don't I get to change my mind of this?

Listen here, I am *not* unreasonable.
It's *my* past, disowned for decades;
now I have the courage to confront it.

Tell me the name of the custodian,
the one who filed this thing away
in the dimness of a storage room,

like the ones behind museum shows,
where the permanent collection waits
for a chance to emerge into the light.

I know my collection's not a beauty;
it traces my skid right off the map:
degree, successful marriage, kids.

So tell me who has shelved my past.
You say I've known it all this time —
the desired name, you say, is mine.

Are You There?

What would my father think
as I squint into a maze of words,
not into a microscope, as planned.

Only child, only daughter of a lawyer,
I was under his keen scrutiny myself.
I was supposed to be a boy, his heir.

We slammed our doors, we screamed.
I hugged his bulk in the Atlantic Ocean
long before he taught me how to swim.

Man of the law, dreamy artist-female:
how on earth did we dare to happen?
Why did we hold on to the hating?

I know him better since we parted.
For two decades I thought of him
and sensed his unexpected nearness.

We survived each others' differences.
He took me with him to his office.
I took him with me into my notebooks.

Forgive, we both repeat that now.
So many years worn out with warfare,
rubbed thin as old threadbare rags.

Never told you, I think I hear him say:
I loved you more that my dream son.
Oh Father, why did we wreck all we had?

Knowing You

Dad, you're there and I'm here,
thinking distance separates us,
but I sense you near me.

As you walk tree-lined streets
on the other side of town
or climb the ancient steps
up to your suite of offices,
I walk away from you.

As you enter that restaurant
where we sometimes dined,
where they knew you well,
where the wine was good,
I eat stew at a shelter.

As you move I feel the effort
when you take the stairs,
when you take your time,
when breathing is hard,
I still want to aid you.

As you water the geraniums
where you placed the pots,
where I watched you do it,
where the sun was right,
now I light a cigarette.

In your beautiful house
you brood like a dark bird.
I've seen you do that before;
as you dwell on mistakes,
I brood about my own.

I'm here and you're there
but I was wrong about this:
distance *cannot* separate us.

Late Again

My father died a week ago; I didn't know.
We hadn't spoken for some twenty years.
I do not like the newspaper's heft.
Life is tough enough, why study death?

It took me decades to forgive my father.
I'm always late for everything; now this.
The angels might deliver news of earth
to the dead, reading the obits in reverse.

So here I stand, unable to move,
too old for tears, too young for relief,
still believing in spiritual resolutions,
holding out for magical conclusions.

And now I turn into an airborne jet,
circling above this house and garden
in a holding pattern, waiting to land
on a field I never mapped in dreams.

She Must Be Joking

"Don't give me a happy ending, it's a cheap joke,"
I tell the blue-eyed social worker named Michelle.
"Don't give me that old bullshit, not this time."
So Michelle snaps back, adjusting her glasses.

"You must be kidding." I feel fizzy, dizzy, drunk.
"About this?" Her stare pins me to the office wall.
"This only happens in a Dickens novel," I explode.
"You, Oliver Twist?" Her laugh shocks me sober.

I come thudding down into the chair beside her desk.
No, she wouldn't take the latest news as a sick joke.
I lean close, as if to whisper during class. "I can't go."
"You can." She stands. "You've been ready for years."

She's right, I know, but I did not want to be ready.
"If I go out on my own again, I'll fail, I'll screw up."
"You'll fail if you don't." Michelle's tone is quiet now.
This gets my attention and I get what she means.

For years I've been respected by the girls at Gilead,
not because of education, privilege, or family ties.
In spite of them, somehow, I became a Someone;
not content, complacent, pleased, but there I did fit.

Now I've inherited the townhouse of my early years.
By a miracle, a fluke, an effort to cancel out his guilt,
my father, a cold man, a hard man, left me this gift,
the first one he'd sincerely offered to his misfit child.

Of course, there's a catch — always there's a catch.
I'd have to enter that house and relive its silent Hell,
meet all the demons waiting there and host every one:
Alice in Plunder-Land, where I was stolen from myself.

I could live there, I suppose, or sell the property away; do something else with it I can't even begin to imagine. There I stand again, stiff as a tree on a windless day, wondering if I would be home here or homeless still.

Wondering if this is Dad's ultimate revenge?

The Test

Going to my father's townhouse
though I swore I'd never do this.

Keys, silvery sticks in my hand.
Locks clicks open for me easily.

Time stops, my vision fractures,
Persian rug asleep in hallway.

Parlor waiting, it holds its breath.
Sofa reclines, chairs sit tight,

cold hearth, no fire, no life here.
Silence around me, smothering.

Clack-clack of my heels so loud;
dining room next, its long table,

shining mahogany, only the best,
like a bier ready to hold a casket.

Too many chairs, maybe fourteen;
long ago celebrations, now dead.

Same kitchen, old-fashioned now,
but white, glaring white, waiting.

I fear those stairs rippling upward
my heels dent their smooth silence.

Upstairs my room, same as always:
canopy bed, old doll resting there.

Master suite, a cave to swallow me;
looking harmless now in frail sun.

White cold tiles in the room of terror;
the bath, its tub empty, holding still.

Sweat streaks my spine as I look:
nothing left, nothing here, no ghosts.

my steps near that tomb-like tub
but she is gone, the girl I once was.

Exorcist, that's who I've become.
Turning on water, I let it run hot.

Rising steam fills this evil room,
blurring it, then erasing its face.

Suddenly I am done, water off,
tub fading, vanishing into air

Now I'm stronger than you are,
I say; this place falls into place.

Again, I walk through the house,
imagining all my friends here.

Roxy, out of her box, Lil alive,
Meg here, not on her grate.

Ma'am from the soup kitchen,
Lulu risen from her grave-bed.

The women of Gilead take over,
lounging, talking, taking baths.

Colors, like snipped crepe paper,
bounce on the air: red, gold, pink.

154

These are the colors of laughter,
rising from the floors, even sinks.

Giddy, dizzy, I force myself out
among the copper-leaved trees

of an autumn weekday, its clarity
etched on the air, twice magnified.

My father is somewhere out here;
I pass through him, offering thanks.

This Must Be the Place

Again I pace my father's house,
imagining my friends are here
settled, strong and living out
what they were meant to be:

The women of two shelters
and many others, far beyond,
living in my father's house,
laughing, talking, washing walls.

Now I know what I want here.
This house must be the place
I've searched for all this time.
It drove me out — now it's mine.

I can make it what it has to be:
Affordable Housing for us all.
But the neighborhood is furious;
my announcement raised Hell.

The unsigned threats come in,
today eight, more graffiti, too.
I feel chilled, caught in shadow.
Sisters, what am I doing to you?

Forget it, the women say, go on.
This will pass, blow off, away,
we'll just stay strong, stay calm.
Enjoy our independence day.

My Father's House

This place was said to be haunted
but a ghost never appeared to me
while I grew up within its dim walls.
My father's beautiful townhouse:
his inheritance from his own father
in a traditional, moneyed, locale,
before it was gentrified, made chic.

I loved this place: its historic air,
tree-lined streets; quaint churches.
Living here was going back in time.
But my father's house had a chill;
he kept the temperature at sixty-six
and he kept his nature cold as well.
I hated the house, loved its street.

Now this hellish house is my own.
I believe its demons have moved on
— if not, they will, if I get my way.
But there are other demons now,
predictable protests; so much rage.
Petitions and threats come each day:
more unsigned hate-mail against us;
our "invasion" of the neighborhood.

Its property values may decline
but there's more to this, I think.
We are seen as lazy, dirty, crazy,
by many of the residents here —
and some of us are, true enough.
And many of us, *many*, are not
like most of my sisters at Gilead.
Civilized, once your peers, we are.
How hard we try to "pass," fit in.

Yesterday I heard gunshots, a few,
probably not to do with the move;
maybe some kid shooting tin cans.
I see graffiti on this shelter's walls;
I fear I've put us in harm's way —
getting above myself again, again.
"We'll get you gone," one note says.
Scare tactics? Or am I paranoid?
Still, we can't give in, give up, delay.

To Joy

I don't trust you; I never did.
You get our hopes too high.
Where are you when they die?

You have tuned the women up,
spinning them into excitement
but I can't live up to you, Joy.

I've gone out with you before
it always ends the same way:
a quick thrill, then a let-down.

I'm suspicious, almost cynical,
after all my years of struggle —-
are you just a one-night high?

You're not like contentment,
steady and sane happiness,
good on gray-haired mornings.

Your color is a garish red to me,
No deep serene and stable blue
or the green of grounded grass.

So bounce like an edgy balloon
rising up to caress the ceiling
dangling your alluring strings

but when you pop like a cork
I'll gather up your shiny shreds
and toss their Mylar bits away.

All right, tell me I'm too uptight,
but I must protect these women
from another disappointment.

Quests and Questions

"You're really sure?" Sister Nan asks me.
"Sure?" asks the social worker, Michelle.
To answer, I take them back to the house.
They study it, they study me — they smile.

Arms linked, we three go back to Gilead.
"It's not that simple," Michelle tells me.
"But it is," says Sister Nan. "Trust me."
"Leave it to my father's lawyers," I add.

Can this be Real Life, I ask myself later,
when my decision has been announced:
Transitional Housing for selected women,
in my old family home — now my own?

Everyone can't go there at one time;
Some women are not ready yet —
They will stay at Gilead nearby.
Nan must shuttle back and forth.

Will this be too much for her, for us?
I know we will have to try it out.
I know somehow this is meant to be.
I have always believed in destiny.

That day Gilead jumps with excitement.
I asked the women: the vote, unanimous.
The neighborhood may not want us, I warn,
there may be protests, even violence —

Lulu shouts: "We been through worse."
Everyone stands up as they start to laugh.
"Can people like us get happy endings?"
I have to ask the question I ask myself.

"Ending?" They shout. "It's only a start."
"You right, girl," Ma'am raps her cane.
"Right you be," the women support her.
But they don't know about the threats.

I sense coming trouble, amid the joy.
This is too fine to be real, I'm thinking.
Something, I feel, just has to go wrong.
I wait for it as I wait for the next night.

Some neighbors gather with us outside:
a small demonstration for "solidarity:"
A growing circle of candle-lit prayers
as I step —

[*Here the notes break off*]

Sister Nan's Notes

9:05 pm, May 2, 1995
Washington, DC.

I am waiting at the hospital. Gunshots broke up our demonstration. Outdoors. Tonight. Peaceful. For support. Some neighbors. Support for our plans. Our move.

Andie Lane — shot in the chest. Gunman a youth, just sixteen. Didn't mean to hurt anyone. So he told police. "Just trying to scare them off." Thought he'd please his father. Who hated our "future invasion." His Dad's gun.

The son fired. Maybe three, four shots. Like firecrackers. I thought. Andie — hit. Kid froze. Police quick. Andie, unconscious, rushed to hospital, surgery. Now in ICU. Docs say her chances 50/50.

The women at vigil outside.

Andie's condition — no change in last two hours. I can't leave. Notes updated as needed.

Sister Nancy M. Brady, N.S.H.
Director, The Gilead Shelter for Homeless women

Author's Notes

The poems in this book are linked by a thematic and narrative thread. They are best read in order of appearance. I used a variety of literary formats to suit the varied material.

Many characters and situations on these pages were inspired by situations I experienced, saw, or heard about from reliable sources. None is a literal, verbatim reproduction.

I deliberately characterized this book's fictional narrator as a woman from a privileged and educated background. I wanted to show that homeless women, narrowly stereotyped, come from all strata of society. Although the majority may be daughters of working-class families, many are not. I wanted to allow the narrator's voice to reflect both education and street parlance, which I have heard melded together.

For about seventeen years, starting in 1985, I was a regular volunteer working with homeless women in Washington, DC. I kept a running log or notebook during that time. At first, I came for the liturgical seasonal of Advent. I stayed many years longer.

Eventually I concentrated on one "day shelter." I was a weekly volunteer at Rachael's Women's Center, originally a Catholic Worker House, for several years. I also volunteered at the Luther Place "night shelter;" at the shelter run by the Committee for Creative Non-Violence; and at a shelter for ill and injured homeless people. I also knew women at the Mount Carmel Shelter and The House of Ruth.

In my time, a downtown Baptist Church offered a

dinner program for the homeless. There were and
are soup kitchens and food pantries open as well. I
went out with the Salvation Army's mobile soup
kitchen and came to know women who slept on
grates; one of many who sleep in their cars; some who
had lived in cardboard boxes under a freeway.

Homelessness is a complex and multi-faceted
situation of vast proportions in America. This book is
not intended to be a sociological dissertation, a
romanticized view or an analysis of the issue:
"decorated messages." I simply wanted to express my
impressions of homeless women.

This book is a work of poetic fiction, so any
resemblances to living persons are purely
coincidental. However, I was inspired by the courage
of many homeless women. I can never forget them.

My special thanks to Pastor John Steinbruck and his
wife Erna of Luther Place, among many others. My
deepest gratitude, affection, and admiration will
always go to the late Sister Mary Ann Luby, longtime
director of Racheal's, a superbly run day-shelter for
many years. Sister Mary Ann was a steller model,
guide and teacher for me as well. I miss her. Thanks
also to Dawn Swann, who became the Director of
Rachael's, and to the many dedicated social workers I
knew in this field.

My grateful acknowledgment to the following books:
    Shadow Women by Marjorie Bard;
    *Tell Them Who I Am: The Lives of Homeless
        Women* by Elliot Liebow,
    A Far Cry From Home, by Lisa Ferrill
    *Beloved Community: The Sisterhood of Homeless
        Women in Poetry,* A W*H*E*E*L Anthology.

No poems from this latter collection appear in my book; its poetry is original.

Above all, I thank the countless homeless women who let me into their lives, thoughts and emotional terrain. I am honored to have been a small part of their diverse and unforgettable stories.

A handful of these poems appeared in some of my previous poetry books and one in my novel *Deadline*.

Many people ask if I found it depressing to work with the homeless. I never did. The women were so varied, as we all are. Most of the women I knew or saw or heard about, had remarkable grit, courage and spirit.

These qualities did not make them saintly; but rather salty, savvy, and often, possessors of amazing faith. Many had a strong sense of sisterhood. No one was "perfect," but who of us can claim to be that?

I found the women compelling, even in their low times, or maybe especially then. They hung on under circumstances that could have defeated many of us. Every time I stood back and watched the women I thought, "That could be me...or any of us."

The homeless women taught me a great deal about the human spirit: its fragility and fallibility, its yearning for dignity, its flashes of grace.

I remember a young woman, an epileptic runaway at the CCNV Shelter. On the anniversary of Dr. Martin Luther King Junior's birthday, she stood in a circle with others who sang, *We Shall Overcome*. Each woman offered a prayer out loud. The runaway lifted her eyes and hands as she cried out, "God, make me Somebody. I want to be Somebody." I can hear her voice today.

Marcy Heidish
September 20, 2016
www.marcyheidishbooks.com

A WOMAN CALLED MOSES

*Houghton Mifflin Co., Original Publisher

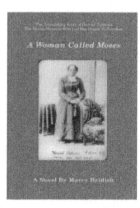

*Award-winning, best-selling novel based on the life of Harriet Tubman, abolitionist and conductor on the Underground Railroad.

*Literary Guild Alternate Selection; *A Bantam paperback.

*TV Movie, starring Cicely Tyson, still available on DVD.

Praise for *A Woman Called Moses*:

Publishers Weekly: "Her story has been told before, but never as eloquently, almost poetically, as here...achingly real...a strong narrative of a totally committed woman, one who speaks directly to our own desperate need to feel committed—and our wish that somewhere in the world there were more people like Harriet Tubman."

Washington Post Book World: "Profoundly rewarding...a daring work of the imagination."

Chicago Sun Times: "Marcy Heidish has, almost uncannily, crawled into the skin and very mind of Harriet Tubman. The dialogue sings with poetic beauty."

Houghton Mifflin Co.: "As events build toward a stunning climax, we are drawn into the spellbinding narrative of an extraordinary life, and a portion of our American past."

WITNESSES

* Houghton Mifflin Co., Original Publisher

* Award-winning novel based on the life of lay minister Anne Hutchinson, <u>America's first female advocate of religious freedom</u>.

* Citations: Society for Colonial Wars; laudatory reviews; large-print, hardcover and paperback versions.

<u>Praise for *Witnesses:*</u>

The New York Times Book Review: "...nothing ordinary about her creation of this remarkable woman. The novel abounds in literary grace. It employs the voices of the times as though heard this minute."

The New Yorker Magazine: "A striking novel...a compelling portrait."

The Washington Post: "Pure pleasure. Anne Hutchinson is real; thanks to *Witnesses,* she at last assumes her proper place in American history." —Jonathan Yardley, Pulitzer Prize-winning critic.

Ballantine Books: "This fearless woman, mother of fifteen, a leader in medicine and politics, comes to vivid life in these pages. A true believe in religious freedom who paid dearly for her principles in two trials for heresy. In the tradition of Arthur Miller's *The Crucible*, Witnesses is the deeply felt portrait of a woman in the paranoid climate of 17th century Boston."

THE TORCHING—*The Book Store Murders*

* Simon & Schuster, Original Publisher

* Acclaimed contemporary novel, in hardcover and paperback.
* Literary Guild Alternate Selection; laudatory reviews.
* Optioned for TV movie.

Praise for *The Torching*:

Washington Post Book World: "Because of Heidish's skill, we get the full force of her double-whammy, in part due to the grace with which she weaves the present-day and the historical, but also because of her inventiveness at the book's close, the daring way she gets both strands of plot to unite... a stylish and intelligent novelist to boot, more than up to the dizzying, tale-spinning task that she set for herself here."

Kirkus Reviews: "Shuddery mystery-suspense with supernatural overtones."

Library Journal: "Intricately constructed. A deliciously spine-tingling, multi-layered literary mystery."

Publishers Weekly: "Subtle, gratifying psychological suspense. Penetrating characterizations...Heidish impeccably orchestrates the historical and contemporary, the supernatural and psychological."

Denver Post: "Macabre ride...Eerie. Intriguing. Frightening surprises...Enjoy."

Arizona Daily Star: "An imaginative, amazing writer...A magician with words."

New York Daily News: "Compellingly readable and likely to induce the screaming-meemies."

THE SECRET ANNIE OAKLEY

*New American Library, Original Publisher

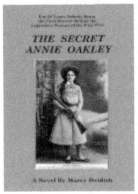

* Acclaimed novel based on the life of the legendary sharp-shooter.
* Hard- and Paperback versions
* A *Readers Digest* Condensed Novel.
* Optioned for film.
*Translated into several languages, laudatory reviews.

Praise for *The Secret Annie Oakley:*

Kirkus Reviews: "An immensely touching and cohesive fictional biography of the legendary sharp-shooter, builds from exemplary research to a fresh portrait of a talented woman in crisis, a class act—as Heidish reconstructs. with color and drama, the choreography of the shows, the tone of the period, and the textures of a haunting past."

The Arizona Daily Star: "...an imaginative, amazing writer, a magician with words. Each character has been brought to life with a mere pen stroke; flesh and blood beings that are more than fiction. A master-piece of creative writing."

The Kansas City Star: "An unforgettable story."

Christian Science Monitor: "...Marcy Heidish weaves historical facts into a novel so moving that there will be many times in the years to come that I'll take pleasure in remembering that stout-hearted woman. 'Annie Oakley' hits the bull's eye every time."

MIRACLES

*New American Library, Original Publisher

* Historical novel based on the life of **Mother Elizabeth Seton**, first American-born canonized saint.

* Main selection, *The Catholic Book Club*.

Praise for *Miracles*:

The New York Times Book Review: "This appealing book, told from the point of view of a skeptical modern priest, moves swiftly through tragedy to triumph."

Kirkus Reviews: "Working delicately with a balance of Church hagiography and psychological insight, Ms. Heidish provides another strong focus on the root dilemma of female saints and achievers."

New American Library: "*Miracles* is the story of an unforgettable woman's life and love. It is a novel charged with the vitality of a life that saw many changes, and with the power of a love that took many forms.[whether] as a lonely daughter of a wealthy, indifferent man; a searching young woman; a contented matron embracing a marriage that produced five beloved children; a widow searching for new meaning to life."

DEADLINE

* St. Martin's Press, Original Publisher

* Contemporary psychological novel with a "mystery" as a narrative line.

* Nominee for prestigious national "Edgar" Award; fine reviews.

Praise for Deadline:

Washington Post: "*Deadline* is a tense, well-turned tale, filled with authentic police and newspaper people. Heidish's taut, punchy style moves the story at lightning speed."

Kirkus Reviews: "The high-tension plot is enhanced by sharply etched pictures, by many vivid characters, and by a crisp, clean, first-person style. Heidish imbues her haunting story and her gutsy heroine with a rare sense of tenderness and poignancy. An impressive mystery by a gifted writer."

St. Martin's Press: "This wire-tight novel probes relentlessly, driving deep into psychological darkness and violent death. As the riveting story reaches its stunning conclusion, we see a complex woman forced to meet the ultimate deadline."

A Dangerous Woman: Mother Jones, An Unsung American Heroine

*A compelling, inspiring new historical novel, another powerful "profile in courage" American-style novel based on the life of Mary Harris Jones, a self-proclaimed Hell Raiser, daring labor leader, and colorful, quirky humanitarian.

*The arresting novel of an indomitable force, dressed demurely in widow's weeds and lace collars who:

> As an Irish immigrant—lost her homeland to the Great Famine.

> As a wife and mother—lost her whole family to yellow fever.

> As a dressmaker—lost home and business to the Chicago Fire

> As a survivor—turned from sorrow to help others survive.

Follow one of America's most feisty, fearless and forgotten heroines whose rallying cry was:

"PRAY FOR THE DEAD—AND FIGHT LIKE HELL FOR THE LIVING!"

DESTINED TO DANCE: A Novel About Martha Graham

> They called her a genius.
> They called her a goddess.
> They called her a monster.

Which title best fits Martha Graham, iconic Mother of Modern Dance? Find out—in the <u>first historical novel about this great American diva</u>.

DESTINED TO DANCE is a creative portrait of the legendary dancer and choreographer. Heidish offers another remarkable account of an American heroine: her successes, her sorrows, and her struggles.

Here is a masterful portrait of Graham, on stage, backstage, offstage. We see Graham's break-through brilliance, often compared to Picasso's or Stravinsky.

We also witness Graham's triumph over alcoholism, despair, and a failed marriage. Set against the intriguing world of dance, Martha Graham's story offers us a close-up on a complex and compelling overcomer.

Martha Graham (1894-1991) invented a new "language of movement," still taught around the world and exemplified in such classic works as *Appalachian Spring*, among 180 others.

As always, Heidish's research is thorough and her sense of her subject is magical. For all who love the arts, all who seek inspiration, and all who like to read between history's lines, *DESTINED TO DANCE* is a must-read book.

Scene Through A Window
A Historical Romance

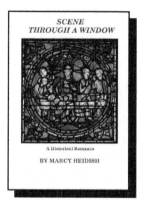

Travel through the centuries to watch a timeless love unfold around a timeless masterpiece: the fabled cathedral of Chartres, France. In 1194, an unthinkable disaster struck that sacred site. In one June night, a firestorm devastated the cathedral, its artwork, and parts of its surrounding town.

Immediately, the finest artists converged on Chartres to plan a new and innovative structure, built to endure and to surpass all that went before. Inevitably, these plans led to plots and rivalry, threatening the realization of a daring and demanding dream.

Against this backdrop, two lovers struggle to conceive the new cathedral's stained glass windows, still regarded as marvels today. This quest centers on discovering <u>new gem-like colors:</u> unique, precious, and <u>incomparable</u>. The pair, under increasing pressure, embarks on an intense search for the mysterious but elusive answers

Deftly weaving fact with fiction, Marcy Heidish sets an inspirational love story against a thoroughly researched Medieval backdrop. With her proven attention to detail, Heidish transports us to the winding streets of Chartres: its sounds and smells, its interiors and intrigues. Suspenseful, engrossing, and imaginative, *Scene Through A Window* creates a magical space where the impossible can happen.

Soul and the City

*** WaterBrook Press
(Random House imprint)**

Praise for *Soul and the City*:

*"I actually started reading Marcy Heidish's *Soul and the City* on a subway train. I must say it had exactly the effect she writes about: it gave me peace in the middle of the hurry, the rush, the loud noise of the city."
—Rick Hamlin, executive editor, Guideposts; author of *Finding God on the A Train*

* "Marcy Heidish has compiled a rich and nuanced touring companion to rival any Michelin or Eye-witness guide—usable in any city of the world. Keep it close and you will meet beauty and holiness no matter where you pause to look."
— Leigh McLeroy, author of *The Beautiful Ache* and *The Sacred Ordinary*

* "*Soul and the City* is a deeply inspiring call to awareness to connection with God and with others, and ultimately to soulful worship through so many aspects of life in the city that we find mundane, undesirable, or that even go unnoticed. Almost instantly, upon delving into its pages, you find your perspective changed."
— Sarah Zacharias Davis, author of *Confessions from an Honest Wife, Transparent, and The Friends We Keep.*

Defiant Daughters

*Liguori Publications.

Praise for *Defiant Daughters*:

What do
Joan of Arc,
    Immaculée Ilibagiza,
      Corrie ten Boom, and
        Sojourner Truth
have in common?

These women are among those whom best-selling author Marcy Heidish calls "Defiant Daughters."

This informative, challenging, and entertaining book spotlights the lives of more than 20 spiritual trail-blazers and their responses to crises of conscience.

They represent different races, denominations, and nations, but all are feisty—often fiery—and always faithful to their callings.

Heidish seeks out the decisive juncture where each took a stand for conscience, however high the cost.

This stunning and compelling book will bring you face-to-face with an unforgettable female gallery of "profiles in courage."

— Liguori Publications

A Candle At Midnight

*Ave Maria Press, Original Publisher

Praise for *A Candle At Midnight*:
* "Heidish honors modern medicine and spiritual healing in this compelling work."

— Alen J. Salerian, M.D., Medical Director of the Washing-ton Psychiatric Center

* "This is not a book of abstractions. I recommend this book to anyone who is caught in the darkness of mid-night."

— Martha Manning, Author of *Undercurrents: A Life Beneath the Surface*:

* "A masterpiece!"

— Rev. Nancy Eggert, Spiritual Director

Who Cares? Simple Ways YOU Can Reach Out

*Ave Maria Press, Original Publisher

Praise for *Who Cares?*:
A lonely neighbor, a colleague in distress, a friend in difficulty. In situations like these we want to reach out and help, yet so often we feel unsure about our response.

What to do?
What to say?
What is enough?
Too much?
Too little?

This practical book is designed to bring out the caring person in each of us. Marcy Heidish offers simple, specific ways to practice the art of caring, especially within our immediate circle of concern: family, friends, neighbors, and coworkers.

Heidish reminds us of the many little things we can do to open the door to a caring relationship.
— **Ave Maria Press**

"Contains savvy insights and wisdom about service. This is an ideal resource for anyone interested in engaged spirituality."
— *Cultural Information Service*

Too Late To Be A Fortune Cookie Writer
"A novelist has a specific poetic license which also applies to his own life."
~ Jerzi Kosinski

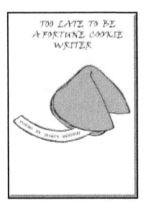

Marcy Heidish, award-winning author of fourteen books, fiction and non-fiction, is just such a novelist with a "specific poetic license."

Her work has been praised for its "lyrical grace" and so it is a special joy to present her first book of poetry. Ms. Heidish has written poems for decades.

With humor and humanity, this collection spans a broad range of subjects. Insight, wit and depth enliven these poems. They address universal concerns: maturity, mortality, memory and much more.

Ms. Heidish gives us an intimate glimpse into a writer's soul. Adept at varied verse forms, she amuses, reflects, recalls, and rejoices:

• "A watched pot never boils unless you're boiling vodka."

• "Houses crowd my life like chairs on a November beach."

• "The sun is a peach, half ripened, at hand." And the poet brings us with her.

BURNING THE MAID:
POEMS FOR JOAN OF ARC

"Joan was a being so uplifted from the ordinary run of mankind that she finds no equal in a thousand years....Her story would be beyond belief if it were not true."
—Winston Churchill

"She is the Wonder of the Ages. And when we consider her origin, her early circumstances, her sex, and that she did all the things upon which her renown rests while she was a young girl, we recognize that while our race continues, she will also be the Riddle of the Ages."
—Mark Twain

Here, in poetry, is a fresh approach to Joan of Arc, that famous heroine-for-all-seasons. Almost six hundred years after she was burned at the stake, Joan's story still compels, fascinates and challenges us.

Credited with saving France, that famous warrior-maid leaps from a new poetry collection by Marcy Heidish, a gifted specialist in historical fiction (*A Woman Called Moses, Destined to Dance*, etc). Heidish's poetic reflections on Joan are riveting, imaginative, and beautifully crafted.

Whether you know a little or a lot about Joan of Arc, this original and elegant collection will invite you to see "The Maid of Orleans" from a wealth of insightful perspectives. If you approach Joan as a role model, a puzzle, or a poem herself, you will find this book an impressive and inspiring read.

WHERE DO THINGS GO?

This luminous book of poems from the award-winning author goes deeper and lighter at once and speaks to the reader in an engaging manner: spirited, sassy and sensitive.

Where Do Things Go? offers fresh reflections on everyday life, expressed with humor, insight, and lyrical grace.

In a conversational tone, Ms. Heidish takes on delight, death, beauty, and the ironies of living.

Rediscover yourself in this poetic mirror for today's adults, challenged by changing times.

Praise for _Who Cares?_:

Kirkus Review, featuring **_Where Do Things Go?_** as one of its **Books of the Month**, described it as "a powerful collection of poetry in which humor is tinged with sadness, and grief is leavened with warmth.... Poems full of linguistic delights and keen emotion."

***

"Ms. Heidish's poems are like little jewels, each with its own facets, depths, and colors, by turns sparkling, reflective, and pensive, set in a musical jewel box that sings with the poet's heart." — Tencha Avila., award-winning playwright.

Short Pieces:

Articles and book reviews published in *Ms.* Magazine, *GEO* Magazine, *The Washington Post*, *The Washington Star*, and various in-flight periodicals.

Two of these pieces are:

* *The Pilgrim Who Stayed,* **GEO Magazine**, about Chartres Cathedral, widely translated.

* *The Grand Dame of the Harbor*, about the Statue of Liberty, was a highly acclaimed cover story for **GEO Magazine**. This article is included in a textbook anthology designed to teach writing to college students. Winner of coveted Apex Award.

See Marcy Heidish page at:

www.Amazon.com

[AND Kindle] *

www.marcyheidishbooks.com

 * Marcy Heidish Books are printed by Lightning Source and distributed by Ingram of Ingram Content Group Inc., the world's largest distributor of physical and digital content, providing books, music and media content to over 38,000 retailers, libraries, schools and distribution partners in 195 countries. More than 25,000 publishers use Ingram's.

INDEX

CPSIA information can be obtained
at www.ICGtesting.com
Printed in the USA
BVOW08s0732080418
512775BV00015B/178/P

9 780990 526254